Resting Place:
Safe Haven

Resting Place Series Book Two

Resting Place:
Safe Haven
Resting Place Series Book Two

Mary M Beasley

LewMar Innovations, LLC
Silver Spring, MD

Edited by Pirkko O'Clock

ISBN: 978-0-9986604-0-0

Printed in the United States of America.

The name of the LORD is
a strong tower; the righteous
runneth into it, and are safe.
Proverbs 18:10

Dedications

This book is dedicated to my Heavenly Father, my Lord and Savior, Jesus Christ, and Holy Spirit. If I had ten thousand tongues, I still couldn't thank You or praise You enough for saving me and transforming my life!

To my children, Cody, Amber, Amir, Marcus, Britmarie, and Lewis, who continue to challenge me to do more and be more, then tell me that they are proud of me! I am so blessed!

To Lewis, my husband, and best friend, the man who makes it his business to fulfill all of my dreams. Next to God, you hold my heart! 1-4-3

To Pirkko, my editor, and friend, truly your pen is like a refiner's fire. Thank you for making my words flow.

Prologue

January 4, 1992

Kevin Weston Jr. sat in the back seat of his father's brand new 1991 Oldsmobile 98, grinning from ear to ear. His dad and mom, Kevin Sr., and Dotty Weston talked about his dad's promotion and about using the extra money to fix up some things around the house. Little Kevin didn't know what a promotion was but thought it had to be good because they had a brand new car. As they drove off the car lot, his mom had tears in her eyes as she thanked God for their new car, something they had never owned. Their old one was sitting in the backyard, waiting to be a blessing to someone. When Kevin's dad asked what they could do with the old car, he heard his mom say, "We are blessed to be a blessing, so let's bless someone with it." Mama was always looking for ways to bless people.

Ten-year-old Kevin Weston Jr. labeled the "old man" because of his serious nature, was glad that he was the oldest of his three siblings,

1

earning him permission to go with his parents to purchase the car. They had left the house early that morning and had been at the car dealership all day. They had stopped for dinner on the way home, Little Kevin eating his favorite Happy Meal. As he leaned to look out the window, Little Kevin couldn't think of a time when he had felt this good; everything was perfect. He stretched out on the back seat, looking at the stars, wondering how many he could count before he fell asleep. Eyes drooping, he started drifting off to sleep listening to his dad and mom talk, thinking how surprised the rest of the kids would be when they saw the new car.

Little Kevin felt his mom shake his leg, and heard her say, "Hey, Old Man, don't fall asleep, we're almost home."

Then he heard her scream, "Kevin! Watch out!" Little Kevin heard his dad, say *Jesus!* Before he could sit up to see what was going on, something hit the back of their car. The car went spinning out of control.

Little Kevin screamed, "Dad! Dad!" He watched with tears in his eyes, scared out of his mind, while his father tried to gain control of the car. Once they stopped, Dad grabbed Mom and asked if she was okay. She was crying but said she was fine.

Then he turned to check on Little Kevin, "Old Man, you alright?" Little Kevin sat up and looked out the back window before answering. He screamed as he watched a big, red truck with the shiny grill coming right at them. His dad didn't see it; his mom screamed right along with him, then everything went black.

Little Kevin woke up to the sound of his name, "Young Kevin? Young Kevin, I need you to unbuckle your seatbelt and get on the floor and be very quiet. Don't say a word. Understand?"

Through his tears, Little Kevin saw Mr. Sam. Something in Mr. Sam's voice and the look in his eyes caused Little Kevin to push down his tears and the pain in his head, unbuckle his seatbelt and get on the floor.

Mr. Sam continued talking in a calm voice, "Young Kevin, someone is coming over, don't say anything and don't move. I'll keep you safe, okay?"

Little Kevin, looked into his eyes, nodded his head and closed his eyes, saying nothing. He heard loud voices yelling, and then they sounded far away as he drifted into darkness.

≈≈≈

Little Kevin woke slowly. He had been fighting to wake up; he had tried a few times, but sleep kept pulling him back. Finally, he opened his eyes to see Grams, sitting by his bed. In a hoarse voice, he called to Grams, trying to reach for her, but couldn't move his arms.

"Kevin, baby, you're awake! Thank you, Jesus!" Grams moved over to the bed, pushing the nurse's button, talking through tears, telling the nurse that he was awake. She kissed his forehead and said, "Thank God, everything is going to be alright. How are you feeling, baby?"

"My head hurts. What happened? Where are Mom and Dad?"

"Kevin, don't you remember the accident?" Grams touched the bandage on Kevin's head, her voice filled with concern, "Oh baby, don't you remember?"

"What accident?" As Little Kevin looked into Grams' eyes, the doctor came into the room and started shining a light in his eyes, causing his head to hurt even more, and asking him a lot of questions. He could hear Grams telling the doctor the he didn't remember the accident, and that he was asking for his parents.

Kevin felt his stomach crunch. Something was wrong; something bad had happened, and he should know about it. Tears ran down his cheeks as he locked his eyes on Grams, "Grams, where are Mom and Dad?"

The pain he saw in her eyes told him before she said a word. "Kevin, they're gone, they died in the car accident."

Chapter 1

Lillian Collin woke up drenched in sweat; *it's just a dream, a nightmare,* she told herself. The nightmares still tormented her. Even after two years of being safely hidden away from Hector, his beating still plagued her dreams. Lillian had to keep reminding herself that she was safe, and Hector Ramos was behind bars. No one would find her here in Resting Place. Taking a deep breath, Lillian remembered what Kevin Weston told her to do after a nightmare. She picked up her Bible and read the 23rd Psalm; *The Lord is my Shepherd; I shall not want. He makes me to lie down in green pastures; he leads me beside the still waters…* Halfway through the Psalm, Lillian began to feel God's presence and peace. Grateful, she whispered, "Thank you, Lord."

Brushing thick, damp, brown curls away from her cinnamon brown face, Lillian looked at the digital clock on her nightstand: three in the morning. Realizing she wouldn't be able to get back to sleep, she got up, went to the bathroom, washed her face, and brushed her hair into a ponytail. Looking into the mirror, she saw the evidence of the violence she continued to relive in her dreams. Though the jagged scar that ran from her left ear along her jawline to the edge of her lip had faded, it was one of the constant reminders of the price she had paid to see Hector Ramos brought to justice for killing her brother Ricardo, for taking away the only family she had left. Her chest burned with pain just thinking about how much she had lost in the last three years. She had to leave Los Angeles, enter a Witness Protection Program, change her name to Lillian Collin, and stay at Safe Haven. It was a high price to pay, but she had paid it, and she would see it through. Shaking off the turbulent thoughts, Lillian dressed and headed to the kitchen.

Walking in the dark through the huge brick house with an open floor plan, Lillian remembered her first impression of Safe Haven; it reminded her of a huge grandma house. The large wrap-around porch, with a long driveway, and white shutters that stood out against the bright, red, brick house. Lillian didn't have a grandma, but she had visited her girlfriend Annie's grandmother's house. Safe Haven made her think of Annie and her grandmother, only Safe Haven was much, much bigger. Smiling at that pleasant thought, Lillian went to the refrigerator and began pulling out breakfast items.

≈≈≈

The safe house had accepted three women late the night before; all three had been severely battered. It always broke Lillian's heart to see what men did to women they professed to love. She had seen her mother abused and later murdered at the hands of a man who claimed to love her. That kind of love left Lillian, the oldest child, alone to raise her little brother, Ricardo. She vowed long ago that she would have nothing to do with that thing called love. She'd been approached many times in school and college by guys asking her out. Lillian would smile and turn them down every time. Her refusals earned her the nickname "Sickle," short for "Icicle." Lillian didn't care about the names; as long as they kept their distance and continued to accept her "no," she was okay with that. Refocusing her thoughts on the needs of the women, she had pushed those memories back into the past, then grabbed sheets and

9

towels, heading toward the women's assigned rooms.

Lillian had worked with the on-call staff to treat the women's wounds while encouraging them that they had made the right decision, letting them know they were not alone and that they didn't have to return to the abuse. She had tried desperately to calm their fears and show them that they were in a safe place. She knew the first few hours in the shelter were vital to their decision to walk away from their abusive relationships. In the past two years, Lillian had talked to many women at this crucial moment; some chose to leave the harmful relationships, while others were too afraid to leave, returning to their abusers. The latter was never a wise choice and often made things much worse for the women who returned.

It was well after midnight before Lillian had crawled into bed, too tired and too late to call Brandy Hart, the owner and cook at Safe Haven. Lillian had hoped she could sleep a few hours, but now that she was awake, she wanted to start breakfast and check the pantry to see what needed to be restocked.

As Lillian turned on the stove, she heard a piercing scream. Shutting the stove off, she immediately ran to the counter and hit the panic button to the police station, one of many located throughout the house. She then ran to where the screams came from, grabbing the phone and dialing 911. "This is Lillian Collin at Safe Haven. I'm reporting screams at the facility; I believe we have an intruder! Please send someone!" The 911 operator spoke in a calm voice, "Ma'am; we have a unit in the area. ETA is two minutes." Running down the hall, Lillian heard another scream coming from the front hall. She stopped in the hall as she saw Janie, one of the new residents, being dragged toward the door.

Without thinking, Lillian focused on the intruder. Running at full speed, she threw herself into the man, knocking them all to the floor. Then Lillian started swinging, punching and screaming her head off. Janie, realizing she had help, began swinging and screaming as well. Lillian and Janie's screams alerted the other two women, who ran into the room, one holding a rolling pin, scared but standing by. When the police arrived, two officers pulled Lillian and Janie off the intruder. As he limped away in handcuffs, escorted by the police, the women hugged each other with tears in their eyes, each one silently communicating their

11

support for the other, saying without words, *I'll fight for you; no one will hurt you again.*

Chapter 2

Lieutenant Kevin Weston was bone tired; he had pulled a double, covering for one of the men who was out with the flu and then spent a couple more hours finishing up paperwork. Heading home, his only thoughts were a quick shower and bed. Then his police radio came to life with a call of a possible intruder at 1001 Cross Roads Lane. Recognizing the address, Kevin whispered, "Safe Haven, Lillian's place." Fatigue forgotten, he turned on his siren and lights, heading for Safe Haven.

As his car sped to the remote location, Kevin's thoughts went back to his first encounter with Lillian Collin. She had been his first case as a Lieutenant. He had received a call from U.S. Marshall Ben Rayns, his dad's best friend, and Kevin's godfather, requesting assistance for a witness needing to be transported to a safe house. Ben informed him that it was an emergency transport and asked if Kevin had the space to accommodate the witness. Kevin accepted the case and took notes while Ben informed him that the witness had received some medical treatment and was stable enough for transport, but would need emergency care upon arrival; their ETA was 7:30 p.m. hanging up the phone, Kevin looked at his watch: 6:30 p.m. He only had one hour to prepare for the witness.

Kevin had called Tate, his brother, former Army medic and Emergency Room Trauma Physician. Tate had joined the safe house responder's team after serving three years of active duty. "Tate, we have a witness coming in who needs medical attention, ETA 7:30 p.m."

"Okay, I'm on my way."

≈≈≈

Arriving at Safe Haven, Kevin had noticed that most of the responder team was already there. Walking into the building, he greeted Brandy Hart, the owner, and her daughter Maggie, counselor and computer support, Trace Kenton, his partner, and Tate Weston, his younger brother. They were ready. Their adrenaline spiked when they saw a train of four plain, black SUVs coming down the long driveway towards them.

Kevin and Tate approached the second car as Ben Rayns got out of and turned to help someone out of the car. Lillian stepped out of the car and fell as her legs gave out from under her. Taking in the black and purple bruises on her face, arms and legs that the summer dress she wore couldn't hide, Kevin's first thought was, *What kind of monster would do this to a woman?* Lillian thanked Ben for helping her and stuck her chin out with determination, assuring him that she could make it. Kevin's second thought was: *What amazing strength she has.* Shaking his head, he ran to the infirmary to get a wheelchair, pushed it over to them, and helped Ben put Lillian into it.

Tate took charge once the woman was in the infirmary; working with skillful speed, assessing her injuries, while Maggie assisted him. They were a very small team of responders; the need for security had caused them to become highly skilled professionals who were crossed-trained in various areas from cooking to reconnaissance. They depended on each other, and the trust they held for one another was without question. Kevin watched Tate call out diagnoses and instructions at the same time. Walking out to check the grounds, Kevin knew that it was going to be a long week.

≈≈≈

Three hours later the patient was sedated and resting in the infirmary. Ben Rayns called the team together to brief them. He sat at the head of the conference table, opened a brown folder labeled "Classified" and began speaking, "Okay, guys; first of all, I want to thank you for your assistance in this case. The woman we have is linked to Hector Ramos. She gave us information that we used to shut down his entire drug operation, something we had been working on without success for the last five years. She risked her life to draw him out of hiding. By the time we got to her, we had to pull Hector off her to make the arrest.

"The woman's name is Monica Sanchez; she made contact with us about a week ago, stating she had information that could lead to getting Hector Ramos convicted. At first, we didn't take her seriously, until she started providing information that was considered to be classified. I scheduled a meeting with her and found out that her younger brother was recruited by Hector's boys and was later killed in a drug deal that went bad. He was sixteen years old. Right before he was murdered, he gave Monica some information about Hector and his operation. Monica's brother was helping a friend who was trying to get out. She believes they found out and killed him. She tried to get the police to arrest Hector, to call him in for questioning, but Hector was so clean no one could touch him. After trying to go through the legal system with no results, Monica took matters in her own hands. She went after Hector, got close to him, and when she had something on him, she contacted me.

"Hector got a tip that something was going down and went into hiding, but Monica risked her life to lure him. We owe her a great deal. Hector wants her dead. Our sources tell us that there is already a price on her head in the six-figure range. She's our only witness; Hector's men have gotten to the others who could testify against him. They are either too scared or dead. That's why we moved her with the minimum medical care. We had to get her out of Los Angeles before anyone could trace where she went. She will stay in the Witness Protection Program, using the name Lillian Collin until

Hector's trial. Her documentation is being prepared as we speak."

Kevin listened to Ben's briefing, thinking, *What was she thinking, dealing with Hector? She could have easily been killed.* Kevin couldn't stop the feelings of admiration he had for Monica's determination and fearlessness and a sensation of protectiveness that surged through him like an electric jolt. Disregarding that unfamiliar feeling, he continued listening, taking a few notes as Ben handed out assignments to secure the facility and their witness.

"Here's the deal, boys, and girls," Ben stated, "we will remain on site for the next two weeks, providing 24-hour one-to-one protection. Let's lock this place down; nobody in, nobody out, with four-hour shift rotations. As soon as Hector was arrested, people started showing up dead. Our job is to ensure that Monica is not one of them. Any questions?" He looked around the table as the team members shook their heads. "Good. Then let's get to our assigned posts and to coin a phrase from a very wise man, 'Watch as well as pray.'"

≈≈≈

At midnight, Kevin was seated in an armchair beside Monica's bed watching her sleep; he doubted that she would wake up, due to the strong medication she had been given. He realized that the average person looking at this five-foot woman, covered with bruises from head to toe, with broken bones and cuts, would think that she was a mess. Kevin saw all the injuries, but he also saw a woman of great strength, beauty, and loyalty. He asked himself how it would feel to have someone love him so much that they would willingly face death for him. He felt a stirring in his heart that he hadn't felt since he was a teenager but quickly buried that feeling, telling himself that he was here to do a job, nothing more. Sitting forward with his elbows on his knees, he began praying for Monica. *Father, in Jesus' name, I lift this young woman up to You for healing and protection. Give us, Your servants, wisdom in protecting her. Heal her body, mind, and spirit, and if she doesn't know You, Lord, draw her into Your saving grace, in Jesus' name, Amen.*

≈≈≈

Kevin's cell phone rang, bringing him out of his thoughts. Looking at the screen, he saw Trace "Cowboy" Kenton, his partner and best friend's name. "Hey, Cowboy, I guess you got the call about an intruder at Safe Haven?"

Trace replied, "Yea, I'm on my way there now. Any idea what happened?"

"No, but I'll know in a few minutes. I just got here." Kevin replied.

"Okay, my ETA is ten minutes. I'll see you there."

Chapter 3

Kevin parked beside a blue and white police car that blocked an old dark blue F-150 pickup and headed into the house. As he entered the foyer, he looked for Lilly. Seeing her across the room, he made a quick assessment to see if she was okay before addressing the arresting officer. "Hey Travis, what do we have here?"

Travis Black was new to the Resting Place Police Department, having joined them eight months earlier. He was an easy going guy who clearly loved law enforcement and had already proven to be an asset to the department. Their captain, Lawrence Smith, had confided in Kevin that he would be retiring within the year and wanted to recommend Kevin for promotion to captain and to take his place. He also discussed promoting Trace and Travis. Kevin hadn't said anything to either of them but knew that those two were good men who served the department well, and he shared that information with their captain.

Travis reported, "The suspect, Roy Grimes, followed Janie Sherman here and tried to get her to leave with him. When Ms. Sherman refused, Mr. Grimes tried to remove her forcefully. Ms. Collin heard Ms. Sherman's screams, called it in and tackled Mr. Grimes. The other residents heard the screams and came to help, but Ms. Collin and Ms. Sherman detained Mr. Grimes until we arrived." Travis smiled as he said, "We had to pull those two women off him."

Keeping a straight face at the picture he got of Lilly tackling Roy Grimes, the six-foot-two-inch linebacker-looking guy. Poor guy, he never knew what hit him. After two years of knowing Lilly, Kevin knew her to be a dynamo with a heart of gold and the strength of a lioness who would not hesitate to jump in with both feet to protect and defend the women who came to Safe Haven. At that thought, pride and admiration filled his heart and that stirring started again. Again he reminded himself that Lilly was a friend, and until Hector's trial, she was his job; he had a duty to protect her, nothing more.

"Thanks, Travis. Read him his rights, and take him downtown. Charge him and lock him up." Turning his attention to Lilly, Kevin saw her talking with Janie. Walking over to them, he heard Janie say, "Lilly, thank you so much! I thought he had me. All I could do was scream."

"That was enough to get my attention."

"Lilly, you've shown me something tonight. Who would have ever thought that the police would be pulling us off of Roy Grimes? Amazing."

Lilly asked, "Janie, are you okay?"

"Yes, I'm better than okay. I got to beat up on the man who's been smacking me a

round for the last three months, and he's going to jail. I'm doing good. No, I'm doing great, thanks to you."

Kevin interrupted, "How are you, ladies?"

Janie spoke first, "Doing great, thanks to Lilly! I don't know what would've happened if she hadn't tackled Roy."

Raising an eyebrow, Kevin looked at Lilly, "Tackled?"

Lilly blushed and looked away. "I didn't know what else to do. It was the only thing I could think of to stop him. I did put in a request for some self-defense classes for the ladies and me staying here."

Shaking his head, Kevin wondered how the conversation had gotten off Lilly's reckless action, and onto her getting some training. He gave her a sober look and said, "He could have had a gun, Lilly. You took a risk tonight." Their eyes met, his dark brown to her light brown, the look saying far more than words.

She lowered her head and said in a quiet voice, "You're right. I'm sorry."

Feeling no joy in being right, Kevin continued, "I'll talk with Maggie and Trace and see if we can arrange self-defense classes. I'll let you know Monday evening."

The smile Lilly gave him caused his heart to quake in his chest. How could a guy guard his heart when just one of her smiles could make him feel things that no woman had ever made him feel? It was times like these that made him want to know her better, but relationships were not for him. Susie had made it painfully clear that he was not the marrying kind; that he only had one love, and that was his job. After making that statement, she began shopping around for the marrying kind, while still dating him. Her betrayal ran deep.

"Hi, Kevin. What happened?" Trace asked while removing his Stetson from his head as he walked toward Kevin. Trace and Kevin were as different as two people could be. Trace was a country boy from Montana, the life of the party, with blond hair almost to his collar, just within regulations. Kevin was very clean cut, with short curly black hair, an every "t" crossed kind of guy, the strong, silent type. They had been roommates at the Police academy and had become friends and partners. Trace's outgoing personality caused him to receive more than enough attention from the female population of Resting Place. Kevin knew that, like himself, Trace didn't date casually; he also knew Trace's love for God and his desire for a mate. On those two things they saw eye to eye and held each other accountable.

Trace had been accepted as part of the Weston family and as Grams' adopted son. He loved the attention he received from Grams. It amazed Kevin the way Trace could become a little kid in her presence, basking in her hugs or praises of his latest accomplishments. A time or two Kevin had thought about being jealous of all the attention Grams gave Trace, but after thinking about it, he realized that she wasn't slighting him. She was just an amazing woman with a capacity and gift to love people right out of their hurt. She did it for him and his brothers and sister. Kevin realized that Grams' ability to love, comfort and encourage was part of her ministry, and he considered her a living example of God's love.

After being briefed about what happened, Trace said, "This is the second incident they've had. I think we need to meet with the team and talk about security here."

"I agree. I'll contact Ben and see if we can schedule a meeting as soon as possible."

"How's Lilly?" Trace asked. Although Kevin hadn't said anything to Trace about his feelings for Lilly, Trace knew Kevin liked her, really liked her. He also knew that as long as she was under their protection, Kevin would not act on his feelings. Trace saw how badly Susie had hurt Kevin when she cheated on him with a fellow officer. Kevin was so devastated, he swore off relationships because of her. Trace also knew it would take a special woman to capture Kevin Weston's heart, and from what he could see, Lillian Collin was that woman. Trace had hinted to Kevin about talking to Lilly a couple of times, but each time Kevin referred to her as his job. Kevin didn't want to talk about Lilly, just like he didn't want to talk about Susie and T.J., and just like he didn't want to talk about his parents. Trace knew that Kevin had chosen law enforcement because he was unsettled with the way his parents died. The case was not resolved, labeled as a cold case, with no leads. Then there was T.J., constantly taking cheap shots at Kevin about Susie. Kevin had started shutting down, introverting, not good. Trace was determined to help his friend, but since he wouldn't talk, Trace resolved to talk to God about it until Kevin was ready.

"She tackled the guy to stop him from taking one of the women." Kevin controlled his tone so he wouldn't show how upset he was about Lilly attacking the man.

"That is one gutsy lady," Trace said with a grin until he saw the look in Kevin's eyes. Clearing his throat, he asked, "Is she okay?"

"Yeah, this time. What if the guy had a weapon? She could have been hurt or worse."

"Kevin, I think you know Lilly well enough to know she'll do whatever it takes to keep these women safe. We might as well train her and the other women who work here so they'll be able to protect themselves."

Nodding, Kevin replied, "She has been asking for some self-defense training."

Trace paused, and then said, "I was thinking more on the lines of our team training."

Kevin frowned and asked, "What are you thinking?" Not waiting for an answer, he went on, "That Lilly become a team member?"

"Yeah, that's what I'm thinking." Trace waited for some feedback, but after hearing none, he said, "Kevin, you can't protect her twenty-four-seven. We need to help her be safe, show her how to protect and defend herself and these women."

After another long pause, Kevin responded, "I'll talk with Ben about it."

Chapter 4

Hector Ramos sat in his prison cell as the doors clanged shut for the night. How he hated that sound, a constant reminder of his lost freedom. He moved to his bed as the lights turned off. Every night at this time his thoughts drifted to Monica, sweet, innocent Monica. As he lay on his bed, he let the hatred and rage course through him. He kept reliving his last night with her, his last night of freedom. His only regret was that the police came before he could finish her off.

How many times had he told his boys not to get caught up with the ladies? Use them then lose them, that was his rule, but as soon as he saw Monica, he had stopped following his own rule. He let her get close to him, for what? So she could betray him. Oh, she will pay for her betrayal, for her lies, and for his lost freedom. That night Hector vowed he would finish what he had started with Monica. She would die a very painful death. That thought brought a smile of satisfaction to his face.

As he drifted off to sleep, Hector went over the plans he had just put in place to take out the power players and send a message to their boys that a new lord was taking over, and that he, Hector, was now the only game in town. Hector alone would call the plays, and their only option would be to play his game or die. With a little chuckle, he rolled onto his side and went to sleep.

≈≈≈

T.J. Muller stared down into his empty beer mug while sitting at his favorite table in McKinney's Bar and Grill, the only bar in town. T.J. was fuming over the rumor he heard around the station about Kevin Weston being considered for the Captain's position. It was bad enough that Kevin made Lieutenant before him; now they were considering making Kevin his boss. No way! The very thought of it made his blood boil. T.J. didn't consider himself to be a racist; he got along with black people as long as they stayed in their place, and he even dated Susie, Kevin's old girlfriend. He smiled at the thought of taking something away from Kevin. He didn't care about Susie; he told himself he just wanted to take Kevin down a few notches. It felt good to point out Kevin's failed relationship. It felt good to cause him pain.

T.J. reminded himself that the rumor about Kevin being promoted to Captain was just rumor. Captain Smith was still in place and hadn't said anything about leaving, but T.J.'s gut told him that it was more than a rumor. If he didn't do something soon, he would be taking orders from Kevin Weston. That thought drove him to his feet, and he headed out of the bar. Checking his watch and seeing that it was 9:45 p.m., T.J. thought that if he hurried, he could stop by his dad's before heading home. It was time to put another Weston in his place. Pulling out his cell phone, T.J. dialed his dad's number.

"Hello," Timothy Muller's gruff voice answered.

"Hi, Dad. It's me, T.J."

"Hello, Son. What's wrong, you drunk? You don't sound good."

"No, Dad, I'm not drunk. There's this rumor going around the station that Kevin Weston is being considered for the Captain's position."

"What!? Are you serious?

"Afraid so, Dad. I wanted to stop by to see what we can do about it."

31

"That boy is just like his daddy; don't know how to stay in his place. And just like his daddy, we'll just have to put him in his place. Come on over, Son. I'll wait up for you."

Chapter 5

B enjamin Rayns was deep in thought while looking over his retirement papers. At the age of 52, he had 31 years of service and felt the Lord leading him to move on. He had been praying about retirement for the last two years, and just a couple of weeks ago he received peace in his spirit about the decision. He smiled to himself as he realized that most people thought of retirement as the end of their careers, but Ben knew that for himself, that would not be the case. God had given him a plan a couple of years before to develop a team of warriors to protect those in the Witness Protection Program. The Lord had provided the structure of the group and the name *Guardian* early one morning during Ben's devotional time.

Ben knew his retirement was near because since that morning, with each passing day he would receive more information from the Lord about the program, or he would meet another resource for the team. As plans for the team unfolded, his excitement grew. For the past few weeks Ben had been praying about the members of the team, and just this morning identified his team leader. Ben knew a number of men who could do the job, but the leader had to be trusted and above reproach, someone who couldn't be bought. Ben had seen firsthand what happened when those responsible for upholding the law, to protect and serve, used their authority for personal gain. The love of money and power had turned the hearts of many men and women in law enforcement, hence the need for the Guardian team.

Over the years Ben had seen the safety of a number of witnesses in the protection program compromised because of leaks in the system. After careful research, he found officers at all levels could be bought or blackmailed. The Guardian Program would be separate from the U.S. Marshals Witness Protection Program, made up of local, handpicked members who knew the area and the people who lived there. The members would need to possess proven integrity so they could be trusted not to sell out to the highest bidder. The government would provide funding for one year to test the effectiveness of the program. If successful, the Guardian Protection Program would be the first of many elite programs. If unsuccessful, the venture would be scrapped. Ben knew this was not his idea; he knew God was leading him in this, so for him, failure was not an option.

The ringing phone interrupted Ben's thoughts. Picking it up, he said, "Hello."

"Hello, Ben, it's Kevin."

"Kevin, I was just thinking about you. What's going on?" Ben asked with a smile.

Kevin hesitated, "I'm not sure. We had another incident at Safe Haven."

Ben paused, "That's the second one in three months. Do you think it might be linked to Lilly?"

"I don't think so, but Trace and I talked about it and think we should meet and discuss increasing security there."

"So, what happened?" Ben asked.

"A guy came after his girlfriend and tried to take her off the premise. Lilly tackled the guy and stopped him."

Kevin could hear the pride in Ben's voice when he said, "That sounds like Lilly."

"Ben, she could have been hurt."

"Kevin, you and I both know that Lilly is all heart and fearless. We also know that our prayers will do much more than our worries. Is she okay?"

"Yes, she is."

Ben knew that Kevin's concerns for Lilly were more than casual. He had seen how Kevin had watched over her, protected her for the past two years. He had also noticed the way Kevin looked at Lilly when no one was around. He realized Kevin's feeling for her had already gone beyond casual or professional duty. Ben had been praying that his godson would let go of past hurts and open his heart to love again. Ben recognized that Lilly was special from their very first meeting. He knew from the moment he heard Kevin praying for her that first night at Safe Haven, that he and Lilly needed each other. Kevin was different around Lilly. She was able to draw him out of his melancholy moods; she could get him to talk and open up. He seemed at home with her. On the other hand, Lilly was like a broken dove, frightened, tense, and so alone. She shied away from all the male team members except Kevin; with him, she seemed at ease, more relaxed. They had formed a comfortable friendship, but Ben believed there could be much more to Kevin and Lilly's relationship.

Ben was there when Little Kevin was born, standing with Kevin Sr., who was a nervous wreck, questioning his ability to be a good father, worrying about Dotty. That night Kevin asked Ben to be Little Kevin's godfather, an honor that Ben took very seriously, not having children of his own. Ben thanked God for his four godchildren and made it his business to be a part of their lives. He loved them as if they were his own, and they loved him. Kevin stopped calling him "Uncle Ben" when he started at the Police Academy. Ben understood the need for more formality, but missed being called "Uncle Ben." Shaking off his thoughts, he asked, "When can we have dinner? I have some free time on my hands and will be in Resting Place for a few days. What's your schedule look like?"

Thinking it over, Kevin said, "Friday night looks good right now. It may be later in the evening, depending on how the day goes."

"That sounds good. I'll be at the house, so why don't you plan to spend the night?"

"Okay..." Kevin paused, "Uncle Ben, what's up?" Concern entering his voice, "The last time I spent the night, we went over your will."

Ben sighed, "I'm sorry I had to spring that on you, but that last undercover case was unstable, and I wanted to make sure everything was in order." He had missed Sidney's wedding because of that last assignment. He hated missing out on walking Sidney down the aisle, giving her away in marriage. Ben had made a vow to himself that he would not miss another major event with his family. "Relax, Kevin, this is different. I want to discuss some career changes with you."

Ben could picture Kevin's frown when he said, "Career changes? What career changes?" Ben laughed, "Nothing to worry about Kevin; we'll talk Friday night. I'm looking forward to catching up with you." Changing the subject, Ben asked, "How are the boys and Sidney?"

Pushing away his concerns, Kevin talked for the next twenty minutes about Sidney, J.P., Marcus, Tate, and Grams, filling Ben in on how and what everyone was doing. Ben sat back in his chair with a huge smile on his face, taking in all the information about the people he loved most, silently thanking God for his family.

Changing the subject, Kevin continued, "Uncle Ben, I need to talk with you about Lilly getting self-defense training. She's been asking, and since this last incident, I'd feel better if she were trained."

Ben considered his words and then said, "I agree. We can provide some classes."

Kevin cleared his throat and stated, "Trace feels that Lilly would be a good candidate for the response team."

Ben waited, sending up a prayer for guidance with this opportunity to talk with Kevin about Lilly. "And you don't think she's a good candidate?"

Kevin let out a frustrated sigh, "Uncle Ben, she could get hurt. You already said she's all heart and no fear. I don't want her to be harmed."

"Kevin, do you feel she's incompetent or would be a danger to the team?"

"No, Uncle Ben, she's far from incompetent. I just don't want to see her hurt."

Ben smiled as he heard Kevin snap at him, and spoke his next words slowly as if he were weighing each one of them. "Kevin, I know that you care about Lilly and want to keep her safe, but God has a plan for Lilly's life, and being a part of the response team may be part of that plan. I think we should pray about it. Can we talk about it again on Friday?"

Considering his words, after a long pause Kevin agreed, "Okay, Uncle Ben, I'll pray about it." Releasing a breath, he asked, "What do you want me to bring Friday?"

"Nothing, I'm thinking about putting some steaks on the grill. 7:00 or 7:30 okay for you?"

"7:30 is better for me. I'll see you then, Uncle Ben." Hanging up, Ben smiled at how easily Kevin had slipped back into calling him "Uncle Ben." He treasured the close connection he shared with Kevin Sr. and Dotty's children. His heart swelled with love for the Weston children as he realized how much he enjoyed being their godfather and how proud he was of each one. Lifting his eyes to the ceiling, he said, "Kevin, you have some great kids. Thank you for entrusting me with them." Ben saw so much of Kevin Sr. in Little Kevin, who was the spitting image of his father, not only in looks but also in mannerisms. Little Kevin was every bit the leader his father had been. Ben knew Kevin Sr. would have been proud of his son; he sure was proud of him. He loved that boy as if he were his own son, and was looking forward to spending some time with his godson.

Chapter 6

God's will for Lilly's life. Kevin couldn't get that comment out of his head. Could God want her in harm's way again? What if she got hurt or killed? The very thought of losing her had his gut crunching in fear. Fear. Was it fear that caused him to keep his distance with Lilly, cause him to discourage her from pursuing her goals? Those questions made him take a good, hard look at himself.

Being honest with himself, Kevin admitted that he cared for Lilly, more than cared for her. He realized that if he allowed himself, he would fall head over heels in love with her. His thoughts drifted to the times that he had held her in his arms after shaking her awake from a nightmare. Then she would relax and settle down as he prayed quietly into her hair, her sweet smelling hair. Holding her in his arms and whispering God's love and protection over her had affected him more then he wanted to admit.

Recognizing how Lilly affected him, Kevin had tried not to comfort her that way, but each time she would end up in his arms. He knew deep down that in his arms was exactly where he wanted her to be. It was during those times, without any effort on her part, she'd worked her way into his heart. He knew Lilly didn't look at him with any romantic interest. She had been scared physically and emotionally and was self-conscious about the scars on her body, especially the one on her face. The scars didn't bother Kevin; when he looked at Lilly, he saw a beautiful, strong, graceful, amazing woman. He saw a woman, not a witness, not an assignment. He saw a woman with light brown eyes who could make him lose his train of thought. Sometimes those eyes could communicate with just a look, and the connection amazed and scared him.

Kevin hadn't considered a relationship with anyone since his breakup with Susie. It was safer being Lilly's friend and protector. Ben's comment made him take another look at their friendship, and he determined that he would spend some time in prayer about it. Reaching for his Bible, Kevin prayed, "Father, I really care about Lilly, and I'm afraid for her. I realize that I haven't trusted You concerning her. Forgive me, and Father, guide me in what to do about a relationship with her. If it's not Your will that we have a relationship, give me the grace to accept Your will."

Kevin had always been direct and brutally honest with God in his prayers. He had learned from his father that God already knew everything, so it wasn't necessary to sugar-coat or dress up his prayers, wasting God's time and his. Kevin's relationship with his Lord was straightforward, not complicated. He didn't always like what God told him or wanted him to do, but he had learned the hard way that His way is best and that it always worked to his own good if he obeyed. Opening his Bible, Kevin asked God to guide him. Turning to the Song of Solomon, he stopped and began to read.

≈≈≈

Lilly walked slowly to her bedroom. She had cleaned the kitchen from top to bottom including the baseboards. She scrubbed the bathrooms, dusted all the furniture, and washed several loads of laundry. She had pushed herself today, and though she was physically exhausted, yet she continued to push, hoping that tonight when she went to bed, she would sleep. The nightmares had gotten less intense over the past two years, allowing her to sleep a few hours each night. That progress quickly changed with the recent break-ins. As hard as she tried, Lilly couldn't shake the images crowding her mind. In her dreams she could still feel the pain, feel fear, and see death pulling at her soul. Lilly hated feeling scared of the dark and being frightened of falling asleep. She kept telling herself that the danger was over; Hector was in prison. He couldn't hurt her again. She could convince herself that she was safe during the daytime when she was awake, but while sleeping, she became Hector's prey all over again. No matter how she tried to see reason or rationalize facts, each night fear chased away reality as the nightmares took over.

Tonight Lilly sat on the side of her bed praying. She had made so much progress; she desperately wanted to be free of fear. She closed her eyes and prayed, "Father God, I am so afraid. I know the Bible tells us that You will never leave or forsake us and that you will not put more on us then we can bear. I can't bear this anymore." Tears ran down her face as she continued, "Show me how to be brave; show me how to fight the demons that torment me every night, in Jesus name. Amen."

Lilly felt a little better, and smiling, she starting getting ready for bed when the phone rang. "Hello."

"Hello, Lilly, it's Kevin."

Lilly's mood brightened when she heard Kevin's voice. "Hi, Kevin. Are you on the way home?"

"Yes, I am. I wanted to check on you to see if everything was okay."

Lilly smiled. Kevin knew about her nightmares; he had prayed her through many nights when she first arrived at Safe Haven. Countless nights Lilly had found herself safe in Kevin's arms while he prayed away the evil that relentlessly pursued her. Night after night Kevin quoted Scriptures, speaking God's promises that weeping may endure for the night, but joy would come in the morning, that God would never leave or forsake her, that God is a strong tower, and that she could run to Him and be safe. Lilly remembered the peace she felt with Kevin, talking about God's love and protection for her. During that time she began to open her heart to the Lord and eventually accepted Jesus as her Lord and Savior. She was still new to this life, and she still struggled with why Ricardo had to die and why she had to become Hector's victim before anything was done to stop him. Her anger ran deep, and she wasn't sure what to do with it.

"I'm good," Lilly said.

"Lilly."

Kevin's voice was quiet, and he only spoke her name. *How did he do that? With one word, he can read me. How does he know?* Taking a breath, Lilly answered, "It's been harder lately; for the last few weeks the nightmares have been bad." Lilly didn't mention that since the last break-in, she hadn't slept for more than a handful of hours.

"Ah, Lilly. Why didn't you call me?" He sounded disappointed.

"I didn't want to bother you. I thought I would be okay." Lilly replied as her voice drifted away.

"Lilly, you're not a bother to me. Please don't feel that way. Call me anytime. You don't have to go through this alone. Okay?"

"Okay, Kevin."

Sensing her hesitation, he asked, "Lilly, can I tell you something?"

"Yes, you can."

"I understand how bad nightmares can be. Remember the night I told you that my parents were killed in a car accident?"

"I remember."

"I didn't tell you that I was in the car with them. I was ten years old, scared out of my mind. I know I saw something that night, but I can't remember, and I still have nightmares about it."

"Kevin, I'm so sorry. What a terrifying experience, and how awful it must be not remembering."

"It is. In my dreams, I'm a kid again, scared, reliving it all over and over again. When I wake up, I can only remember a part of that night. I know I saw something important. I wake up when my mom screams, and that's the last thing I remember."

"Kevin, that's so devastating. How did you cope? How did you handle the nightmares?" Lilly asked, remembering her prayer for help with her nightmares.

The compassion and caring in Lilly's voice cracked open another part of Kevin's heart. He had only shared this part of his life with his family, not even Trace knew all that had happened. He had no plans of sharing all of this with Lilly, but there he was spilling his guts, and it felt good, right. "At first I would wake up screaming and crying. Grams would hold me and pray for me until I fell asleep."

Lilly interrupted, "Like you did for me?"

"Yes, like I did for you. As I got older, Grams told me I had to learn to fight. She told me the devil walks around seeking who he can destroy, but through Christ, I could resist the devil, and he would flee. She taught me what she calls 'fighting Scriptures' and showed me how to pray."

Lilly was hanging onto his every word., "Did it work? Was it hard to do? Which Scriptures? What did you pray?"

Kevin laughed. She was firing off questions, something he noticed she did when she was excited and interested in a subject. Smiling, he continued, "At first, I was so scared — remember I was just a kid. This was pretty heavy stuff for a kid. Then Grams gave me a visual. She reminded me of when my little sister Sidney got a new basketball for her birthday. I walked her to the playground to play with it. I left her there while I went to ask some of the other kids if they wanted to play. When I got back, some bullies were trying to scare her and take her ball. Sidney was pretty frightened, but once she looked over her shoulder and saw me, she got bold and told those boys to leave her alone, or her big brother would make them leave her alone. I was always tall, and I was twice their size, so they took one look at me and ran away. Grams said when we use 'fighting Scripture,' it's like Jesus our big brother is standing right behind us. She told me to be bold and even loud because Jesus is backing up what I say. Once I understood that I could fight and got a lot more sleep."

"Wow! Kevin, that's amazing, and it really worked?"

"Yes, it did, from that day on. Now the nightmares still come, but I don't have to give in to fear. Lilly, I know it won't be easy, but until you resist the devil, he won't flee."

Lilly asked in a soft voice, "Kevin, would you share Grams' 'fighting Scriptures' with me?"

Kevin's heart melted. The trust he heard in her voice made him feel ten feet tall. Swallowing the lump in his throat, he replied, "Yes, Lilly. I'll share. I'm almost home if you stay on the line until I get to my room; we can go over them."

"Thanks, Kevin!"

The next hours passed as Kevin shared Scriptures and more of his youth with Lilly. She talked about her younger brother Ricardo and some of the good times they had together. She hadn't talked with anyone about Rico. It hurt too much, but with Kevin, it felt good to share about her brother. At 3:00 a.m. Lilly couldn't hide her big yawn.

Kevin smiled, "Somebody needs to get some rest."

"Okay, Kevin." Lilly sounded hesitant.

Hearing her concern, he asked, "Do you want me to pray for you now?"

Lilly let out a sigh of relief, "Please." Kevin began praying, and she felt herself begin to relax. Holding the phone to her ear, she slipped down under the covers, his voice wrapping around her like a warm hug. She felt safe, protected, cared for. When he finished praying, Lilly yawned again, and then whispered, "Thank you, Kevin. Goodnight."

"Goodnight, Lilly."

She hung up the phone, already beginning to drift off to sleep and for the first time in weeks, not worrying about what the darkness would bring.

≈≈≈

Kevin sighed. He had to be at the station in four hours for a morning meeting with Captain Smith regarding an internal investigation, yet he was wide awake and couldn't get the goofy grin off his face. He had just had the best time, talking and sharing with Lilly. He knew he would be extremely tired at the meeting, but he didn't care. He wouldn't change a single second of his time with her.

After the recent break-in, Kevin had waited before calling Lilly, hoping that she trusted him enough to call when she needed him. He had told her to call if the nightmares returned, but after a couple of days, he felt compelled to check on her. She was the most stubborn, beautiful, amazing woman he knew, and he couldn't help being concerned about her. He had to make sure she was okay.

Kevin had altered his schedule a few months after she arrived at Safe Haven so that he would be traveling home when she was preparing for bedtime. Each evening he had called and talked about her day and prayed with her. He always smiled when she yawned and whispered a sleepy "goodnight" to him. Hers was the last voice he heard at the end of each long day, and it was the highlight of his day. As time passed, he called every other day, then once a week. Then he stopped, feeling that the calls were more for himself than Lilly. He knew she didn't have any romantic feelings for him, so he pulled back. However, those calls had become an important part of his day, and Lilly an important part of his life.

Tonight she was different; her faith that Jesus was the answer to the nightmares amazed him. She was excited to receive the Scriptures, asking him questions about how to pray, what to say, when to pray. He gladly answered every question, knowing that she needed to fight for herself, and he was glad she was ready to try. Tonight Lilly was engaged, laughing and even joking with him. Kevin's heart was overwhelmed with love for her. She had awakened a longing in him that had been buried so deep he had forgotten what it was like to feel, really feel, and now his heart was beating again. Kevin headed for the shower, determined to get a few hours sleep. Twenty minutes later, as he settled down and was beginning to drift off to sleep, he still had that goofy smile on his face.

Chapter 7

Friday night at 7:29 p.m. Kevin knocked on the door of Ben Rayns' three bedroom rambler. He smiled, thinking about all the weekends he and his family had spent at Uncle Ben's — fishing, camping in the backyard, watching football and basketball games. Uncle Ben had stepped in when Kevin and his siblings lost their parents and became a father figure for them. He was at every game and event they had; he was there cheering them on. He took Sidney to the Father-Daughter dance and on her first official date. Kevin remembered how hurt Uncle Ben was when he found out that he couldn't attend Sidney's wedding, and the pride he felt when Uncle Ben asked him to stand in for him and give Sidney away. As a young boy, Kevin didn't understand the level of Uncle Ben's commitment to the Weston family, but as a grown man, he could see how much Ben Rayns had sacrificed for them. Kevin loved Uncle Ben as a son loves a father and knew his brothers and sister felt the same way.

Ben opened the door, "Come on in, Kevin. I'm out back at the grill. Why don't you leave your bag by the steps and grab a cold drink and join me."

"Sure, Uncle Ben," Kevin replied as he dropped his duffle bag and grabbed a soda, heading outside. He was surprised to see the table set with fine china and a linen tablecloth. With a raised eyebrow, Kevin asked, "Are we expecting a guest?"

"No. Brandy stopped by earlier today to drop off some paperwork I requested. I mentioned that you were coming over, so she volunteered to set the table. I guess her idea of setting a table is a little different from mine."

A huge grin split Kevin's face as he asked, "Brandy huh? Is there something going on with Brandy that I should know about, Uncle Ben?"

Ben felt his cheeks heat up, but he refused to deny his feelings for Brandy. He had always tried to set an example for his boys, and that included how they treated women. He had taught them to always respect females, and that when they had feelings for someone; it wasn't a crime to share those feelings. That advice had earned him plenty of man-to-man conversations, but it had also kept his godsons out of a lot of female trouble. Ben guessed it was time to live out that example and share his feelings for Brandy with Kevin. He hoped that it would help Kevin share how he felt about Lilly. Ben determined he would not let this opportunity slip by.

Ben's feelings for Brandy ran deep; she was everything he could want in a wife. They had been friends as far back as elementary school. He cared about her all through school and had fallen in love with her in high school. By the time he got up enough nerve to ask her out on a date, she was already seeing Thomas Hart. Ben remained friends with Brandy until she and Tom became engaged., Realizing he cared too much to stay around and watch Brandy live her life with Tom, Ben enlisted in the Army and went overseas. When he found out about the abuse Brandy and her daughter, Maggie had suffered, he regretted not telling her in high school how he felt. He vowed that if given another chance, he would not let fear keep him from showing Brandy that she was a jewel, one that he would treasure all the days of his life.

Ben cleared his throat and replied, "I've loved Brandy for a long time since we were kids. She was hurt so badly in her marriage to Tom that she's afraid to trust again, but I'm patient, and I won't let her slip away without trying."

"Wow, Uncle Ben. I never knew how much you cared for Brandy."

"You were too young, but I talked with your dad about it. He told me that I should tell her before I left for the army. I should have listened to him. Your dad was a wise man."

"Does Brandy know how you feel?"

"She might suspect. I asked her to have dinner with me tomorrow night."

Kevin sat on the edge of his seat, listening to Uncle Ben. "Smooth, Uncle Ben! What did she say?"

"After what seemed like an internal debate going on in her beautiful, redhead, she said yes!" Ben said with a huge smile. "I got a date with Brandy! God is a God of second chances, and I'm glad about it!"

"That's great! I'm happy for you, Uncle Ben. I really like Brandy. I'll be praying for you both," Kevin replied with a smile.

"Thanks, son. Your blessings mean a lot." Ben said, humbled that Kevin's approval meant so much to him. Kevin was truly the son he had never had.

They ate for a while, making small talk about the family and work. When they were almost done, Ben asked, "Have you prayed about Lilly?" He saw Kevin blush and look away and added, "Lilly, huh? Is there something going on with Lilly I should know about, Kevin?"

Kevin had been daydreaming about Lilly earlier that morning when Trace mentioned her name, and that goofy smile had appeared again on his face. Trace had picked right up on the smile and teased him the rest of the day. Kevin knew Trace would be happy for him if he asked Lilly out, but he didn't want to talk with Trace about her. Kevin wanted to talk with his Uncle, Ben. "Lilly and I talked last night."

Ben studied Kevin's face before asking, "About the classes?"

"I've set up some advanced training classes in Self Defense and scheduled some time on the shooting range for her."

"So is she considering joining the Response Team?"

"She was really excited when we talked about it last week. I wasn't in a big hurry to do it, but after our conversation, I prayed about it, and I think it would be good for her. I told her she could train but couldn't work with the team until after Hector's trial was over."

"So who's doing the training?"

"Maggie is taking the lead on this. She has already started; her first class was last Wednesday night. Maggie will work with her for the next few weeks and then Lilly and Maggie will teach self-defense training to the women. Maggie said Lilly is a natural."

"That's great news, so why do I hear a 'but'?"

"No buts, I called to check on her. I was concerned that the recent break-ins may have triggered her nightmares."

"Did they?"

"Yes, they did, but I told her how I coped with the nightmares when I was younger, and she was excited about how I did it and asked a ton of questions. I think she's going to be okay."

"So is everything okay, or is there more that I should know?"

"Afterwards we read the Bible, and I gave her some Scriptures. We just talked about our families, and she told me about her brother. I told her about my parents. Uncle Ben, it felt good; it felt right with her."

Ben smiled, seeing his oldest godson opening his heart to love again. "So you care about Lilly?"

"Yes, I do, but I've always cared about her. This is different."

Ben paused, looked Kevin in the eyes, and asked, "Do you love her, Kevin?"

Kevin looked back at Ben for a long time, and then replied, "Yes, I love her."

Ben couldn't stop smiling as he reached over and patted Kevin on the shoulder, saying, "I'm glad, son. Lilly is a wonderful woman. I really believe God has put you two together. My only advice to you is, if you really love her, don't let her go."

Kevin flashed that goofy smile, "I won't let her go." Feeling at peace with the idea of loving Lilly Collin after talking with Uncle Ben, he knew he could move forward and begin his pursuit of her. That thought brought an even bigger smile to his face. They sat in a comfortable silence, each with their own thoughts about how to win the hearts of the loves of their lives.

Then Kevin broke the silence, "Oh, I almost forgot. What about this career change?"

"The reason I wanted to talk with you is that I'm getting ready to retire."

"Retire? Really, Uncle Ben? How old are you, 49, 50? Aren't you too young to retire?"

"I am 52 years old, and I started pretty young, so I have my years and the age to retire. God is leading me in a new and exciting direction. I've been approved to implement a protection program that is not linked to the Marshall's Office. He slid a file folder over to Kevin which was labeled "Guardian Protection Program."

Kevin gave him a curious look, "What's this about?"

"That's what I want to talk to you about; it's the Guardian Protection Program. Take a few minutes to read over this while I do the dishes." Ben started clearing the table while Kevin focused on the Guardian folder.

≈≈≈

Saturday morning, Lilly woke up to the smell of coffee and bacon. She yawned and stretched before throwing back the covers and getting out of bed. The past two nights she had slept through the night. She had also talked with Kevin the past two nights. Kevin had called from his uncle's house, and they had talked into the wee hours of the morning. She was falling for Kevin Weston. Lilly had always trusted him and cared for him, but now she was thinking of him all day and couldn't wait to get his call at night. Last night before he said goodnight, he asked if she was okay with him calling when he got off work. She was so surprised that he might want to talk with her that she asked: "To check on me?"

There was a pause before Kevin replied, "Yes, I want to check on you, but I also enjoy our conversations. Is that okay?"

Lilly swallowed the lump in her throat and replied in a soft voice, "It's okay."

Kevin let out the breath he was holding and said, "Good, can we pray together before we say goodnight?"

"Sure." Lilly held the phone to her ear, listening to Kevin pray for the women at the safe house, his family and his friendship with her. At the end, Lilly was so relaxed, that she yawned and again said a sleepy goodnight. As she drifted off to sleep, she thanked God for her friendship with Kevin. She had never known anyone like him, and he enjoyed their conversations. She cautioned herself not to read too much into his words, but her foolish heart had already fallen.

≈≈≈

Fully dressed, Lilly looked at herself in the bathroom mirror. She looked happy; she found herself smiling at the woman in the mirror. It dawned on her that for the first time in a long time, she wasn't afraid and she wasn't hurting. As she walked out of the bathroom, turning off the light, she realized that she hadn't examined the scar on her face. She hadn't even noticed it. Smiling, she headed for the kitchen.

"Good morning, Brandy." Lilly greeted her friend as she walked in the kitchen. "Can I help with anything?"

"Good morning, Lilly. No everything is almost done, but I would love to chat with you over a cup of coffee."

Lilly answered with a smile, "I would love that, too."

Brandy reached across the table and touched Lilly's hand. "How are you doing, baby?" The caring and compassion Lilly saw in Brandy's eyes warmed her heart.

"I'm good."

Brandy smiled and said, "I've been praying for you for some time now. I know you've been through a lot, and there has been a great deal of pain in your life. Brandy paused before saying, "Lilly, God wants to heal your heart today." Lilly had a puzzled look on her face. Brandy continued, "May I share my story with you?"

Lilly nodded her head, and said, "Yes."

Brandy took a deep breath and let it out. Then she began, "I had to get married when I was eighteen. My boyfriend took advantage of me one night in the back seat of his car, and I got pregnant. Tom didn't love me; I think he only dated me to get back at someone who really liked me and I liked. Our parents made us get engaged, and we got married when he graduated from college. I had to leave college because I was sick a lot in the beginning and missed a lot of classes. After Tom graduated, he went to the Police Academy, and when he finished, he accepted a position here in Resting Place." Lilly noticed a distant look in Brandy's eyes as she continued.

"For the first few months, everything was okay. I knew Tom didn't love me and resented marrying me, but we were working it out, or so I thought. About a month after he became a police officer, he started coming home drunk. I wasn't used to seeing people drink. My parents and none of my friends drink. Whenever he was drunk, he would yell at me and blame me for trapping him in our marriage. I quickly learned that I couldn't reason with him drunk, so whenever he was like that, I would leave the room. That only made him madder; he starting grabbing me and tossing me around. If I pulled away from him, he would slap me. The slapping turned into punching me in the stomach or chest, then the face. He would threaten to plant drugs on me, then arrest me and take my daughter away from me. This went on for five years."

As Lilly listened, her heart broke for Brandy. She couldn't imagine being treated so cruelly. Silently praying, she reached for Brandy's hand offering comfort without words.

"Tom hated Maggie and me. I tried to make sure Maggie was locked in her room before he came home at night. I never knew his work schedule or any of his business. He wouldn't talk to me about anything. That was our life. I made sure there was food when he got in. Some nights he would come home, change clothes and leave again without saying a word. On those nights he would come back drunk, yelling at me for ruining his life. He'd slap me around a little before heading to his room and slamming the door. A lot of people knew what he was doing, but no one helped me. They were afraid of Tom, so they did nothing."

Brandy hesitated before confessing, "Lilly, during that time, I died inside. I hated that this man raped me and that I was forced to marry him. I hated that he beat me and yelled and screamed at me and told me it was my fault. I hated Tom and everyone who knew about the abuse but did nothing. And I hated God because I believed He hated me and let this happen to me. The only reason I didn't kill myself, and I thought about it, was Maggie. She was my only reason for living."

Lilly thought about her one beating and wondered how Brandy had survived daily beatings. With tears in her eyes, Lilly continued listening as Brandy poured out her hurt.

"On Maggie's birthday, June 5th, I had taken her to the park and bought her some ice cream. Tom never came home in the daytime, so I was surprised to see his truck heading to the house. I grabbed Maggie and told her that we had to get in the house and that she had to lock herself in her room and not make a sound. We made it to the house, but Maggie wasn't in her room when

Tom slammed open the door, drunk and yelling."

Lilly sat on the edge of her seat.

"Something had happened to him; he looked scared. His eyes were wild, and his anger was at a level I had never seen before. I knew we were in trouble. Tom was looking for something, throwing things around, pulling drawers out onto the floor. Then he looked at Maggie; she must have made some noise. He started after her. I told her to run to her room and lock the door. Then I got between him and her. Tom hit me, knocking me across the room. Afraid for Maggie, I got up and jumped on his back. I wrapped my arms around his neck and prayed to God to keep him away from my child."

Lilly was so caught up in Brandy's story she didn't realize she was praying, out loud, "Please God. Please, God. Let them be okay." Brandy gave her a tearful smile and continued.

"Once Maggie was in her room and had locked the door, he got even madder and turned on me. He beat me down to the floor and then stomped on me. As I lay groaning on the floor, I heard his phone ring. He answered it and then ran out of the house. Maggie waited a little while after the door slammed shut, and then came out of her room. Before passing out, I told her to call 911 and tell them that her mommy had fallen and was really hurt and that she was by herself. I told her to open the door when the ambulance came."

"Three days later, I woke up in Resting Place Memorial Hospital. I was told that Tom had been killed in a car accident, drunk driving. He wrapped his car around a tree."

Lilly's tears were flowing. With her hand over her mouth to try to stop words from spilling out she said, "Brandy, I am so sorry. I'm so very sorry."

"Thank you, but that's not the end of the story. I healed up physically, and Maggie and I were okay, but we both suffered with nightmares, anger, and unforgiveness. I started going back to church and went back to school to finish my degree. I really thought we were okay. About a year after I got out of the hospital, the Lord told me He wanted to heal my heart, that I had to forgive and let the anger go. He told me that the nightmares were the enemy tormenting me because I refused to forgive."

Brandy reached over and touched Lilly's hand and said, "Lilly, God was right. He had told me many times to forgive, but I wouldn't

listen, until one night when I sat up with Maggie
because of the nightmares. God spoke to me
again and said if I didn't forgive Tom, Maggie
wouldn't forgive him either, and we would
forever be bound to Tom. That thought horrified
me; I didn't realize that I was still linked to Tom
through unforgiveness and that I had only
healed on the outside. I needed to forgive Tom
and everyone I held responsible for not helping
me. I also realized I needed to ask God to
forgive me for blaming Him for what Tom did. I
also Him to help me forgive myself. The day
that I forgave, truly forgave, Lilly, God healed
my heart. Baby, let go of the anger, hatred, and
unforgiveness. God wants to heal your heart."

Tears streaming down her face, Lilly said, "I
don't know how to let go."

Brandy got up, hugged Lilly and said, "I can
help you if you're ready."

"I'm ready."

As the two women prayed, Lilly began
releasing the anger, hatred, and unforgiveness.
Brandy hugged her as she cried and prayed;
tears flowed as she surrendered her emotions to
God. Brandy could hear Lilly whispering to
God, and thanking Him as each release came.
After she finished praying and the tears

stopped, Lilly was quiet but still holding on to her friend, her head resting on Brandy's chest. Lilly didn't move; at that moment Brandy's arms felt like heaven to her. She had not been held like that in so long, not since her mother held her, and she was reluctant to end their embrace.

Brandy loosened her hold on Lilly when she stepped back, whispering, "Thank you, Brandy. I can't tell you how much your help means to me. My heart doesn't hurt anymore."

Brandy looked into Lilly's eyes and smiled, "You are so welcome, baby. Thank you. I needed to tell my story. I used to keep it to myself, ashamed of what had happened to me. I didn't see that God could use my mess to help anyone, but every time I share it, someone receives a blessing, and I receive one as well."

Lilly replied, "God knew what I needed to hear. I'm so grateful." She paused and looked around the kitchen until she saw the clock. Realizing it was still early, Lilly continued, "My brother, Ricardo was a Christian. Our mom was, too. She used to take us to church and taught us how to pray, but I didn't believe God loved us because our dad would come home and hit our mom. I didn't understand why she would serve a God who didn't protect her. Ricardo was still kind of young, so he didn't see as much of the abuse as I did. When our dad was drunk or high, he would hit mom a few times and then leave the house." Lilly sighed and continued.

"Then one day he came home late at night, it was almost midnight. Mom had sent us to bed and said she wanted to pray for a while. That wasn't unusual. Sometimes when something was troubling her, she would pray all night. Dad's yelling woke me up. I could hear Mom trying to calm him down. I saw him hit her, but this time he kept on hitting her. I grabbed the phone, ran into Rico's room, locked the door and called the police. When the police and ambulance got there, Mom was dead, and dad was gone. The police picked him up about a week after that and charged him with murder. He's in prison now. What little faith I had in God died that day. I had just turned eighteen; Rico was eight, so I assumed guardianship of him.

"Rico loved church, and his friends were there, so I kept going until he could go on his own. During his first year in college, he told me that his best friend Corey was hanging with some guys offering him a chance to make a lot of money. Rico said he thought it was illegal, but he wasn't sure. A few weeks later, he told me that Corey was in some real trouble and asked me to pray for him. Then Ricardo started coming home late, and he was acting funny. A few days before he died, he told me that he was trying to help Corey get out of the gang he was in. He told me about who was in charge and how they were recruiting college kids. Rico said that he and Corey would be leaving the area the next day to get away, and once they were safe, he would contact me and the police. Rico told me if anything happened to him that I should tell the police everything about the gang.

"I was scared and said he should tell the police and let them help Corey. He told me that it was too late and that the only way he could get the information was to join the gang. He told me that Corey didn't know what he was getting into, and he felt led by God to help him get out. Rico tried to talk to me about God, but I was too scared and too angry about Mom to listen. He told me not to worry if anything happened to him because he would be with Jesus and Mom. He said if I really accepted Christ, we would all be together one day. That was the last time I talked with him. He didn't come home the next day, and the day after that I got a call that he was dead." Lilly wiped tears from her eyes. She whispered, "He knew he might be killed and wanted me to be okay."

Brandy hugged her again, "Oh, baby, I'm so sorry, and you've lost so much. I know it hasn't been easy, but God was there all the time. I know you don't see it now, but God was with Rico, and He will be with you. He promised He will not leave or forsake you."

Lilly sighed, "Now I really believe that. I really believe I can trust God, and that He won't leave me no matter what."

Brandy's phone rang causing them both to jump, and then giggle, as Brandy answered, "Hello."

"Hello, Brandy. It's Ben."

"Hi, Ben. What's up?"

Lilly had seen Brandy talk with Ben many times over the last two years, but today she seemed different. Was she blushing? Then Lilly remembered that in her story Brandy had mentioned someone she cared for. As she walked out of the kitchen, she heard Brandy asking where they were going for dinner. Lilly wondered if Ben Rayns was that someone.

Chapter 8

Ben felt as nervous as a schoolboy on prom night. He had faced hardened criminals and even death a couple of times and hadn't broken a sweat. Tonight his hands were clammy, his stomach was in knots, and his heart was beating out of his chest, all over one five-foot two-inch, beautiful, red-headed woman. She was an amazingly strong woman. After Tom's death, she went back to school, earned a nursing degree, and took a position at Resting Place Memorial.

After he was discharged from the service, Ben reconnected with Brandy, and he counted himself blessed to have her friendship. When her mother died five years ago, only a year after her father had passed away, Brandy asked him about turning their home into a safe house for abused and battered women. Brandy told him she wanted to help women who couldn't get help otherwise. Ben liked the idea right away, and when she shared that she wanted to work with the program, he was sold. Together they established Safe Haven. Ben wanted nothing more than to spend time with Brandy; they had worked together for the past five years.

Ben had to admit that he spent more time in Resting Place, not only to see his godchildren but also to be near Brandy and Maggie. Lately, he had found himself longing for far more in his relationship with Brandy, what he could have had long ago if he had taken the chance and told her how he felt. He loved her then, and he loved her now, and he wanted to be with Brandy Hart forever. Tonight he would be laying all his cards on the table, and it was a terrifying thing. He knew they were good friends, but could Brandy feel more for him? Ben felt he had wasted enough time, and tonight he would begin what he prayed would be a lifelong process of wooing the woman he loved.

≈≈≈

Brandy changed clothes for the fourth time, asking herself if she had any decent clothes to wear. What was wrong with her? She was as nervous as a school girl. *Get a grip Brandy; it's just Ben. We've been friends forever. Who was she kidding? She had always cared for Ben Rayns.* All through school they had been study buddies; by the time they were in college she had fallen in love with him. How many days had she wished that Ben had asked her out instead of Tom? How many times had she mourned what could have been, if only... Well, tonight she would enjoy what she considered to be her very first date in 25 years. She decided on a dark green, A-line dress that accented her slim waistline and reached just below her knees. She had worn it at the previous year's hospital Christmas party and had been told that the color looked nice on her. She remembered feeling good wearing it, and someone had commented that the green complemented her hair color. Satisfied with her choice, she hurried to get into the shower. Brandy heard the doorbell ring as she was putting on her lipstick. Taking a deep breath, she said, "Okay, Lord, here we go."

Ben was about to ring the bell again when Brandy opened the door. He just stared, taking in what he saw. She was always beautiful, but tonight she was breathtaking. Clearing his throat, he said, "Hi Brandy. You look amazing."

Blushing, she bent her head, not missing how handsome Ben looked in his navy blue suit. His hair was trimmed, his dark brown curls trying to behave. Ben's hair was the first thing

Brandy had noticed about him. In school he had worn it longer, often running his fingers through it to keep in out of his face. She had dreamed of running her fingers through it, and that memory made her smile as she replied, "Thanks. You're looking very handsome tonight, Ben." Feeling a little embarrassed to say it out loud, she continued, "I wasn't sure what to wear since you didn't mention where we're going."

Ben smiled, "Thank you for the compliment, and as I said before you look amazing, and where we are going is a surprise. Are you ready?"

"Benjamin Rayns, when have I ever liked surprises?" Brandy tried to keep a straight face but failed as a smile broke through.

Ben offered his arm. As Brandy took it, he said, "If you don't like it, we can leave."

Ben had thought long and hard about where to take Brandy for their first date. He wanted to impress her, but he also wanted to spend some quiet time with her. He had called an old college friend of his who owned a Christian jazz dinner club. He knew Brandy liked jazz, and they would have a private table so they could talk and really get to know each other. Ben was determined to be transparent about his feelings and his intentions for Brandy. He just hoped and prayed that Brandy had or could have feelings for him one day.

The jazz venue, private dining area, and the handsome Marshal all added up to the most incredibly romantic night Brandy had ever experienced. She found herself reaching under the table to pinch herself to make sure all this was really happening to her. Was she reading his actions correctly? What could he possibly see in her? Tom's words broke through her thoughts. *Worthless, that's what you are. You can't do anything right. No one wants a no count woman. Hell; I wouldn't have married you if your parents hadn't threatened to report me.* All she could hear was *not worthy, and worthless.*

Ben studied Brandy's expression with concern. "You okay?"

Ignoring his question, Brandy asked, "What are we doing here, Ben?"

Ben hadn't anticipated being transparent so soon about his feelings. Stalling for time, he said, "We are having dinner."

Frustrated, Brandy leaned forward and spoke in a harsh whisper, "Benjamin Rayns, don't act like you don't know what I'm talking about. Why are you playing with me? You've never had any feelings for me, but you bring me to this place. Look, I know no one wants me. I don't know why you brought me here. I thought we were friends." Brandy hung her head as tears began to fall.

Ben reached out and covered her clenched hand and waited until she looked up. Their eyes met. In a calm voice Ben said, "Brandy, you are wrong. I've always had feelings for you. I've always thought you are an amazing, beautiful woman. I wanted to ask you out but was afraid, and by the time I got up the nerve to ask, you told me you had a date with Tom. Soon after that, you were engaged. That's why I joined the Army. I've regretted not asking you out ever since. You asked me what we're doing here." Ben's voice softened, "I'm doing what I should have done years ago. I'm letting you know that I really care for you, beyond just being friends. I'm asking if you would be willing to give us a chance."

Brandy couldn't believe her ears. Her heart was racing. How could this be? No one had ever wanted her. Tom's words were ringing in her head. She just stared with surprise and an uncertain look on her face. Then she heard another voice saying; *Tell him your story, you can trust him with your heart.* Recognizing the voice and realizing that this was the second time that day she would share her story, she whispered under her breath, "Okay, Lord." Squeezing Ben's hands, she smiled. "Ben your words are the nicest I have ever received. I am so flattered by them, but before you make a decision about me, I need to share my story with you."

Ben didn't release her hand; he just sat quietly waiting for her to continue. "First of all, I want to thank you for tonight. It's so special to me because it truly is my first date. The first time I went out with Tom, he raped me." Ben's brown eyes changed to almost black as he clenched his mouth, holding back the rage that coursed through his body.

Taking deep breaths, Ben listened to everything Brandy wanted to tell him. Listening about the mental and physical abuse she had endured ripped his heart apart; he wanted to hit something, somebody. He was filled with a rage he had never known before. He prayed *God help me hear it all; help me be here for Brandy.* As he prayed, Ben was able to say, "Brandy, I'm so sorry. If I had known, I would have protected you and Maggie. I'm so sorry that happened to you."

After Brandy finished, she felt fairly sure that Ben would reconsider his feeling for her, so she said, "I'll understand if you don't want to see me again."

"Brandy, I think you're the most incredible woman I've ever known, and now that I've heard your story and realize why you married and what you've been through, I want a relationship with you, more than ever before. I want to love you and protect you and spoil you. I want to be here for you. Brandy, I do want you, and I have for a long time."

"Ben, I don't know what to say! No man has ever cared about me. It's hard to believe that you do."

Ben listened, his heart hurting because of the pain and doubt that Brandy experienced at Tom's hands. Along with the hurt, he was experiencing a deep longing for her. He wanted to give her the world, show her the world. He wanted to pull her close and love her hurt away, but he knew it wasn't time for that. He had to tell her and keep on telling her until she believed him. He knew in his heart that God had created this woman for him, and he would treasure her for the rest of his life.

The waiter came and left the check. After Ben had finished paying for their dinner, they walked to the car. Ben opened Brandy's door and helped her in. When he was in his seat, he looked straight ahead and said, "Brandy, I really care about you. If you have no feelings for me, I'll accept it. Just tell me now."

Brandy opened her mouth, but she couldn't lie to him. She was scared, but couldn't reject the chance, no matter how slight, of being loved. She whispered, "I want to try, but I'm scared."

Ben turned to look at her, and the affection she saw in his eyes warmed her through and through. He reached across the car and cupped her chin in his palm. "Oh Brandy, I have always wanted you." Moving slowly toward her, Ben lowered his head to kiss her. He didn't want to scare her, but the moment their lips touched, he was lost. Moving his lips over hers, she was still, and then slowly, sweetly, Brandy kissed him back. Her kiss was the sweetest thing he had ever tasted. Gathering his willpower, Ben pulled away from her, giving her one last gentle kiss. He said, "Brandy, we can move as slowly as you want. Will you give us a chance?"

Brandy leaned back in the passenger seat, touching her lips, blushing and wondering who was that girl kissing Ben Rayns. She had never liked kissing. Tom's kisses had always hurt. What she had just experienced was amazing, sweet; it was even tasty. Never had she experienced that. Is this how it felt when someone cared about you? Brandy smiled, "Yes, I want to try, Ben."

Ben reached over and took her hand, bringing it to his lips and kissing her knuckles. "Thank you, Brandy. I promise you will not regret it." The ride home was quiet and comfortable. Ben walked Brandy to her door, gave her a hug and a gentle kiss before she walked inside. As he turned toward the car, he heard her say, "Goodnight, Ben."

"Goodnight, Brandy." He replied as he walked to his car with a big smile on his face, making plans for his next date with Brandy.

Chapter 9

Early Sunday morning, Hector Ramos sat at a picnic table in the prison yard. Every few minutes one of his men would walk up, sit down and report on tasks he had assigned them. Hector's top priority was to find Monica Sanchez. So far no one had located sweet Monica. Two years had passed with no sign of her. His time was running out, with the trial a few months away. His attorney had stalled a few times, but he knew the judge would not grant another continuation. Hector knew as long as he was a threat, she would stay hidden, but what if he wasn't a threat? What would she do if she thought he was dead? A sinister smile formed on his lips as his next visitor approached and sat down.

Hector spoke before the man had time to say anything. "Find me a man in this place who looks like me, same height, build, hair color. Once you find him let me know. Tell the boys to stop whatever they're doing. This is my top priority."

The man stood and walked quickly over to the group of men in the far corner of the yard. Satisfied with his plan, Hector whisper to himself, "Soon Monica, very soon…"

≈≈≈

One week later, Kevin and Trace walked into the Resting Place Police station late Sunday afternoon. Captain Smith had called them in for an emergency meeting in his office. Kevin's mind had been on the past week's conversations with Lilly. She had told him about her time with Brandy; saying it was hard forgiving the people who had taken so much from her and hurt her, but once she did it, she felt free for the first time. He had asked her about things she would like to do after she left Safe Haven, and if she would leave Resting Place. He was pleased when she had said that Resting Place was the only place that felt like home. She had added shyly that she felt safe in Resting Place and with him. He couldn't help the smile that had crossed his face, nor the desire to see her that rose up in him. Feeling his way, Kevin had asked, "Lilly, would you like to have dinner with me?"

"Kevin, that would be so nice, but you know I can't leave the safe house." She had sounded disappointed.

"Lilly, we can have dinner there. Ask Brandy if we can use the small conference room with the flat screen T.V. I'll bring the food and a movie. We can have dinner and a movie tonight if you want."

"Okay Kevin, that sounds great! What time? Can I do anything? Maybe I should cook." Kevin had smiled as he listened to her ask questions in rapid fire mode. Lilly had been excited, a very good sign. He loved to hear the excitement in her voice. They hadn't seen each other since they started talking on the phone a little over a week ago. Now his desire to see her and spend time with her almost overwhelmed him. Her enthusiasm about their date pleased him to no end. He was so focused on what Lilly would like to eat, the movie she might like to see, and the thought of spending time alone with her, Kevin didn't see T.J. Muller walking toward them. T.J. bumped Kevin's shoulder hard, saying, "Watch where you're going, Weston."

Before Kevin could answer, Trace replied, "You watch it T.J. You walked right into him.

What are you doing, trying to pick a fight? You know Captain Smith's rule about fighting." Normally, easygoing Trace would have made a joke about what happened, but today he was direct and commanding. He made sure everyone in the room knew that T.J. had started this. When they all stopped what they were doing and started staring at them, T.J. scowled, muttered something and walked away.

≈≈≈

"What was that about, Trace?" Kevin had a puzzled look on his face.

Trace shook his head, "I don't know. Something's not right with that guy. The Holy Spirit put me on high alert with him. The last time I felt like that we were about to walk into an ambush."

"I don't know what's up with him either, but after that near ambush, I'll always listen when you get a Holy Spirit alert." Kevin patted him on the back.

Trace gave Kevin a serious look. "Kevin, watch yourself with T.J. He's been like a bull in a china shop ever since the word got out that you might make captain when Captain Smith retires. That man has a problem with you, and it has nothing to do with your skills and everything to do with the color of your skin."

"I know he's been heated with me ever since I made Lieutenant before him. I think that's the only reason he started seeing Susie. I hope she figures out that he really doesn't care about her before she gets really hurt. I know there's a case about him and a couple of guys are being reviewed for possible profiling. Captain has been keeping it quiet, but it doesn't look like they'll be with us much longer after the investigation. Until then, I'll follow Uncle Ben's advice, watch and pray."

Trace smiled and said, "Good. Now let's go see what Cap wants."

≈≈≈

Knocking and walking in the door of Captain Smith's office, Trace said, "You wanted to see us, Captain?"

"Yes, come in and shut the door." Kevin and Trace sat down at the small, round conference table. Pulling out a notepad, Kevin looked over as another knock sounded on the door.

"Come in," Captain Smith's voice boomed. Ben Rayns walked in the room. Kevin and Trace exchanged curious glances. Ben sat at the table and pulled a folder from his briefcase. "We have just received a report that Hector Ramos was found dead in his cell."

"How did he die?" Kevin asked.

"The report indicates that he was beaten to death by a gang he had threatened to take over. They believe he was beaten and then dumped in his cell."

"Did they identify the body?" Trace asked.

"Yes, they did. Every inmate was accounted for. Only one prisoner was released, and that happened the day before. Hector was in his cell that morning. When he didn't show up for lunch, and nobody saw him in the yard, the guards went looking for him. They've shut down the facility to investigate what happened."

Smiling, Kevin said, "Well it's over now, Lilly can finally live without fear."

Ben looked skeptical. "Yes, she can, but I want to keep her close for a little while longer. There is still an assigned hit out for her. This sounds too easy. Hector had so many connections even in law enforcement that I find it hard to believe that it's over just like that. My gut tells me we should wait and proceed with caution."

Kevin answered, "I agree, but once word gets out about Hector being dead, the media will run away with that bit of news. We should keep her out of the public eye until things die down. But can she leave the safe house? I have a feeling Lilly won't want to stay hidden too long if Hector is really dead."

Ben replied, "I understand. I'll talk with her and let her know my concerns. I think she could leave, but only with an escort, and she should wear a disguise. We'll keep her out of the public eye until we're sure it's safe for her to come out. I'm on my way out there now to talk with her. Care to join me?"

Kevin said, "Yes, if we're done here, Captain?"

Captain Smith responded, "That's all for the day. I'm sorry to have disturbed your weekend. Kevin, I'll need to see you first thing tomorrow morning. Internal Affairs is sending someone to brief us on the investigation. The meeting is scheduled for 7:30 a.m."

"I'll be here, sir." Kevin, Trace, and Ben walked out of the office happy about telling the news about Hector to Lilly. Kevin knew she would agree to using caution, and he planned to be her escort until Ben determined it safe for her to come out of hiding. Kevin told the other men that he had a stop to make, and he would meet them at Safe Haven. He needed to pick up dinner and a movie and wanted to bring Lilly some flowers–roses, pink roses, even if he had to get a few from Grams' flower garden. This was a special day for a special lady, and he wanted to celebrate.

Chapter 10

Kevin hoped that Ben and Trace had already left by the time he got there, and he could start his date with Lilly. No such luck, they looked right at home when he got there, bags in hand. Lilly met him at the door, with a beautiful smile that just about stopped his heart. Wow, her smile reached her eyes and those honey brown eyes captured his, and the rest of the world disappeared. Kevin was lost until he heard Ben clearing his throat and Trace coughing.

Busted, looking over Lilly's shoulder, Kevin saw Uncle Ben and Trace both with big grins on their faces. He had been caught gazing into Lilly's eyes. A few emotions ran through his mind at that moment. All these he wanted to process later that evening when he was alone, but for now, he needed to get those guys out so he could be alone with Lilly. Leaning close, he whispered in her ear, "Sorry, Lilly. I guess I got caught staring at a beautiful woman." He almost laughed as her eyes got big and her cheeks turned even redder than before. Kevin handed Lilly the bags with their dinner and the movie. "Can you take this in the conference room; I didn't get enough to share."

Lilly nodded with a relieved smile and went off down the hall. Kevin walked into the living room and greeted Trace and Ben. Neither bothered hiding their smiles. Kevin finally said, "Come on guys, don't embarrass Lilly."

They both looked a little contrite as Ben said, "Sorry, Kevin. We're just happy for you."

Trace joined in, "I hope we didn't run her off. Maybe I should go apologize to her."

Kevin looked a little uncomfortable and said, "I'll let her know after you guys leave."

Trace always had a way of reading his moods, as he picked up on Kevin's words. "Leaving? Ben wanted to discuss our escort assignment."

Sensing Kevin's growing frustration, Ben offered, "I'll work up a schedule, and we can meet here tomorrow night at 6:00 p.m. to discuss it with Lilly."

Trace looked from Ben to Kevin and responded, "Okay, well I guess we'll head out. Tell Lilly we said goodbye." As they all headed for the door, Ben lingered behind, whispering, "Enjoy your date with Lilly."

Kevin smiled, closed the door, and headed for the conference room.

≈≈≈

Dinner started a little awkwardly, but Kevin was determined not to let a little embarrassment ruin his first date with Lilly. So he drew her out with questions about her day. He talked about his day. They discussed Hector and what her life would look like now that he was no longer a threat. By the time they had coffee and apple pie, they were laughing about a movie Kevin has seen a few months before. Lilly put the movie in the DVD player, commenting on the fact that it was a romantic comedy. They settled on the love seat in front of the TV.

Lilly was in heaven. It had to be heaven; nowhere else could feel this good. She had enjoyed dinner, realizing how closely Kevin listened to her. She had only mentioned once that she liked grilled chicken and broccoli and apple pie. Tonight she had a favorite meal with the greatest guy in the world. It was almost unreal how happy she was. Sometime during the movie, Brandy came in and cleared their table and turned the lights out where they'd had dinner. There was still plenty of light, and it just felt as if they were in their own world. The movie ended far too soon. Kevin got up and reached for Lilly's hand, saying he should go home. It was clear that neither one of them wanted to end their first date, but Kevin knew he needed to move slowly with this relationship thing with Lilly. As they walked hand in hand, Kevin stopped before opening the conference room door and turned to Lilly, saying in a low voice, "I really had a great time Lilly. Do you think we can do this again?"

Lilly leaned in to hear him, and answered, "I had a great time too, and I would like to do it again."

"Would you like to have dinner Friday night? I have off that evening."

Lilly smiled and then looked concerned, asking, "Kevin, are you sure you want to do this with me?"

Kevin reached out, and placed his hands on her arms, looked into her eyes and said, "I am very sure. I want to see you again Lilly, and spend time with you." With that, he drew her close to him, lowered his head and kissed her.

Lilly stood still, not knowing what to expect. She had never been kissed before and had no idea what to expect. As it turned out, once Kevin's lips touched hers, she automatically responded to him. *Wow, so this is what it's like to be kissed.* It felt natural to respond to him. Kevin was showing her a side of herself that she had not known existed. She wasn't afraid or anxious; she was excited and warm all over. Kevin's kiss was gentle and seeking; it was drawing her in.

Kevin only intended to give her a gentle kiss, but her response took him by surprise and pulled on his heart. He had never felt like this before. He pulled back, ending their first kiss, resting his head against hers, and whispered, "Wow." He looked into her eyes and said, "Lilly, I really care about you and want to court you."

"I care about you a lot, too, Kevin."

He gave her a gentle kiss and said, "Oh, I left something in the car for you. Wait right here. I'll be back in a minute."

Lilly was in a wonderful daze, standing in the conference room looking around, wondering if she would wake up and discover she was just dreaming. A soft knock on the door let her know she was not dreaming. Kevin stepped in with his hands behind his back and said with a shy smile, "I wanted to get you something nice for our first date. I didn't want to give it to you earlier because the guys were here." Realizing he was rambling, he handed her the pink roses.

Lilly stared at the beautiful bouquet, too moved to say anything. *How could he have known that she loved pink roses?* Deep down in her heart of hearts, she had longed for someone to care enough to give her pink roses. Looking into Kevin's eyes, she responded, "Kevin, they're beautiful! Thank you so much." Standing on her tiptoes, she kissed him on the cheek. She turned to go to the kitchen to put the flowers in a vase.

Kevin touched her arm and said, "Lilly," he gazed in her eyes, shaking his head as if he was trying to clear it, he said, "It's getting late." Then their eyes met again. "I'd better go. I'll call you when I get home to pray and say goodnight." He tugged her close for a lingering kiss; they held hands as she walked him to the front door. "I had a great time. Goodnight, Lilly."

"Goodnight, Kevin." Lilly watched him through the window as he walked to his dark blue GMC Yukon truck. When he opened the driver's door, he turned around and smiled at her. Lilly's heart leaped in her chest. Okay, she thought, her fate was sealed; she was in love with Kevin Weston. Cleaning up the conference room, she found herself reliving the wonderful evening with him. Forcing herself to focus, she wanted to be finished cleaning before he called. Smiling as she wiped off the countertop, Lilly headed upstairs to her room.

≈≈≈

Monday morning driving into work, T.J. couldn't shake the anger surging through his body. He was fed up with this waiting game and time was running out. The rumors were sounding more like fact than rumor now. Kevin Weston was in line for the captain's position. T.J. knew that job should be his; they all knew that he was the better man for that job. For heaven sake, couldn't they see that Kevin was black? Why couldn't he stay in his place? T.J. was sick of them all. He would have loved to have gone a few rounds with Kevin yesterday, and knocked that smile right off his face. It would have felt great, but Trace got in the way. Oh, he would take care of Weston soon enough; then he could get rid of Susie, too. Be rid of them all. T.J. smiled as he put on his lights, pulling over a young, black man driving a black BMW, turning onto Peace Drive. T.J. got out of his car, determined to work off some of his frustrations.

"I need you to step out of the car," T.J. said as he approached the car.

"Is there a problem, officer?" Investigator Brian Townson of Internal Affairs asked.

"Just get out the car, boy." T.J. snapped at him, raising his voice.

"Officer, it's highly unusual that a driver is asked to leave his vehicle, why are you asking me to get out of my car? Are you charging me with something?"

Just as T.J. put his hand on his gun and leaned in to say something, another police car pulled up, and Kevin and Trace came out of the car. "Is there a problem, T.J.?" Trace asked.

"No problem. Just a routine check. I'm done here." Walking away to get in his car, T.J. pulled up beside Investigator Townson's car, stared him down, and drove off.

Kevin and Trace walked to the car, Kevin asked if the man knew why he was being stopped.

Investigator Townson struggle to control the anger. "Yes, I have an idea, but I want to share it with the appropriate authorities. Thank you for your assistance, Officers Weston, and Kenton. I'm sure this may have played out very differently if you hadn't showed up." Investigator Townson drove directly to the police station.

At 8:50 a.m. Kevin headed to Captain Smith's office; the 7:30 a.m. meeting had been rescheduled to 9:00 a.m. Kevin took advantage of the free time to have breakfast with Trace. He knew Trace wanted to know about what was going on with Lilly. Trace had been hinting around about her for the last few days. After yesterday at Lilly's, Kevin knew it was only a matter of time before the questions came. So it didn't surprise him when they sat down for breakfast that Trace asked, "So, what's going on with Lilly?"

"Why do you ask?" Kevin replied with a smile.

"Because you're different. Nothing seems to bother you these days, and you have a really goofy smile on your face. I saw the way you and Lilly were looking at each other yesterday."

Kevin couldn't hold back the smile that covered his face. Trace looked at him and said, "That's the smile! What's going on, Kevin?"

Kevin lowered his voice and said, "Lilly and I have been talking."

Trace just stared, then smiled, "As in, 'I like you, you like me' talking?"

Kevin blushed and looked down in his plate, saying, "Maybe."

Trace waited until Kevin looked up before saying, "Hey, Kev, I'm happy for you. Lilly's a wonderful woman. You guys are good for each other."

Kevin smiled and said, "Yeah, I think we are. Last night was our first date, and it was amazing. It's so easy to be around her, and I really like her, more than like her."

Trace grinned, "It's about time! You're not getting any younger."

Kevin gave Trace a serious look and said, "I know, and I don't want to waste any more time. I asked Lilly if I could court her. It's taken me a long time to get to this point. Enough about me; how about you, Trace? When are you going to ask Maggie out?"

Trace knew that Kevin had picked up on his feelings for Maggie. There were very few people who could see beyond the easy-going guy that Trace displayed every day. Kevin had long ago breached that wall. Over the years the two had formed a bond that allowed them to trust one another with their lives, and that sometimes meant getting into each other's business and challenging one another. Trace had done that for Kevin when Susie betrayed him. He was there for him, listening, encouraging, challenging him to keep moving, telling him that God had a better plan for him. Trace was right. God has blessed Kevin beyond measure in his new relationship with Lilly. Now it was Kevin's turn to challenge his friend to reach for what he couldn't see. It was time to get in his business.

"I don't think Maggie wants anything to do with me," Trace said, sounding a little defeated.

"Trace, Maggie has been badly hurt, and I think she's afraid to trust any man. Uncle Ben shared a little bit about how Brandy and Maggie were living with an abusive man. I won't share anymore, it's her story to tell, but I know she cares for you, Trace. Outside of Ben and me, you're the only other male she allows to work with her. I think if you took the time to really let her get to know you, she would let her guard down, and let you get to know her. I'm just saying."

Trace looked thoughtful. "I had no idea; she seems so confident, sure of herself," he said with a mixture of surprise and anger about what he was hearing.

His friend, seeing his reaction, patted Trace on the shoulder and replied, "You guys are a lot alike. There is so much more than meets the eye in you two. Trust God and try, Trace."

"I hope you're right. Pray for us. I think I'll try another approach." Trace answered.

Looking at his watch, Kevin said, "Hey, I got to go. Meeting with Cap. See you later."

≈≈≈

Knocking on the door, Kevin heard the Captain's loud, bass voice, "Come in." As he entered the office, Captain Smith started talking. Never one to beat around the bush, he said, "Kevin, I believe you've met Investigator Townson, although not formally. Investigator Townson headed up the profiling investigation. He came to brief me on his findings, but it seems he ran into some trouble while heading to the station this morning. Investigator Townson, Lt. Kevin Weston will be replacing me as police captain in the next few months. I want him involved with as much as possible during my transition. I know you've briefed me on some of your findings, and I need you share that information with Lt. Weston."

Investigator Townson opened a thick folder labeled classified, cleared his throat, and began speaking. "This investigation was initiated based on three high profile complaints. One of the victims is the son of a congressman, another is the son of a dean from a local college a couple of towns away, and the third one is a youth pastor from a large church in the Richmond area. There were several other complaints, but these three involved physical contact that required medical treatment. These victims have also filed charges of police brutality.

"The victims targeted were African Americans, upper middle class, with fairly new cars, well-dressed, articulate, and they were either visiting or passing through Resting Place. All three reported being pulled over by Officer Muller, who demanded they exit their vehicles. Once out of the vehicle, each reported that Officer Muller attacked them with his fists, while his partner stood by with his weapon pointed at them. After the attack, the victims were left on the side of the road.

"I personally experienced similar treatment from Officer Muller this morning when he pulled me over. He walked up to my vehicle and demanded that I get out the car. When I questioned why I saw him reaching for his gun. I truly believe he would have forced me to leave my car and would have attacked me if Officers Weston and Kenton had not happened on the scene. I was more equipped to deal with Officer Muller than his other victims because of this investigation. However, I'm glad it didn't come to that. The reason we haven't picked up on this case earlier is because until recently, the complaints have just been harassment. The latest three attacks involved assault that happened within the last thirty days, and Officer Muller has been identified as the attacker in each of the cases."

Chapter 11

Walking from his apartment to the soup kitchen on Redemption Lane, Samuel "the Ghost" Alexander, director and counselor for the Resting Place Table, marveled at how his whole life had been transformed by God. He remembered living on these streets; homeless, drunk, not caring about anybody or anything, after watching his team, his friends nearly wiped out in Desert Storm because of him. He had been the team leader; it was his job to look out for them. He had given up, but God hadn't given up on him. He whispered, "Thank you, Jesus," at that thought. No sir, God had a plan for his life, and that plan landed him at the soup kitchen, right in Martha Rose's path.

Martha Rose, affectionately called Grams, was all of five foot tall and maybe weighed 100 pounds. She was a force like no other he had ever known. She drew him with kindness and love, and before he knew it, he was in a Bible study. Grams would give him counseling sessions, but she didn't call them counseling, she would just walk up to him and ask if he had a few minutes for a little chat. In those little chats, Sam would spill his guts and afterward wonder what made him do that. No matter how many times he said he would not share his past, his hurts, each and every time Grams had him alone, they prayed, and the floodgates would open. He poured out his heart to that woman. Sam had never met anyone like her. Grams was like God's agent, her hazel eyes seemed to look into his soul and read him, all of him. What amazed him was that she loved him; she actually loved him. He could feel her love, and it was that love that drew him to God.

Six months after Grams had started her little chats, she pulled Sam aside and told him it was time for him to have a reckoning with God. She talked to him as if God were speaking through her. She told him God wanted to use him for His glory, and it was time to choose. That day, on January 4, 1992, Samuel Alexander gave his life to Christ.

Sam didn't realize that the fourth of January was also the day God would give him his first assignment, to watch over young Kevin Weston. That night Sam was as sober as any preacher, and he saw who hit Officer Weston's new car.

Seeing young Kevin looking out of the car window, Sam knew he had to act quickly. He ran over and saw that young Kevin was the only survivor in the vehicle. His military training kicked in as he told the young Kevin to get out of his seat, on the floor, and not to say a word. Sam promised him that he would protect him. Young Kevin looked up at Sam with trust in his eyes before passing out. Sam had to keep him safe until the ambulance came. He knew the police officer, Thomas Muller, had seen the same thing he saw, and Officer Muller was smiling as he sauntered to the car. Sam was code-named "the Ghost" for his ability to appear out of nowhere. Muller was surprised to see Sam standing by the car when he approached it. For the first time, being a drunk and homeless gave Sam an advantage, and even though he was neither drunk nor homeless, thanks to Grams, he played the role and played it well to keep young Kevin safe. Sam stumbled and then tried to stand up straight, slurring his words; he asked Muller, "What's your business here soldier? Sarg says no one touches this package until he clears it." Muller was so angry Sam knew he would have shot him if the ambulance had not been so close. Sam kept his promise to young Kevin that night; he kept him safe.

Over the years Sam watched over young Kevin and prevented a few attempts on his life during the first few weeks after the accident. When word got out that Kevin didn't remember anything from the accident, the attempts decreased, and eventually stopped. Sam knew the day would come for him to share what he had seen the night of the accident. Lately, the Lord had given him a heavy burden for Kevin. He concluded that he would talk with Kevin when he came to volunteer on Saturday, just to check in with him. Sam knew Kevin didn't remember that he was at the accident, but all of his senses were alerting him that trouble was about to break out and that Kevin needed to be as equipped as possible to deal with it.

≈≈≈

Suspended! T.J. was furious. How could they do that? His morning was finally getting better; he and his dad had come up with a plan to get rid of Kevin Weston. It was a good plan, and they could make some money on the side. Yes, his day was getting better, until he got a call to report to the Captain's office. He was surprised to see Weston sitting at the small conference table, and shocked to see the man that he had pulled over that morning. From there, things just got worse. T.J. couldn't believe that he was under investigation for profiling and police brutality. He almost laughed when Captain Smith asked for his badge and gun. Confusion, then shock, then rage flashed through his mind when Captain Smith said he was on suspension until Internal Affairs met next week. As he handed in his badge and weapon, his anger only escalated when he asked why Weston was in the room and was informed that he would be assuming the captain's position in a few months and needed to be aware of the investigation. It took everything in T.J. to clamp his mouth shut and walk out of that room. As he proceeded out of the front door, ignoring the curious looks, his anger grew with every step. Who does Weston think he is? Pulling out his cell phone, he dialed his dad.

"Hello," Timothy Muller answered with a curt, no-nonsense voice.

"Dad, it's me." T.J. released a frustrated breath, finally allowing some of his anger to seep out.

"T.J., what's wrong?"

"Weston's in charge and I've been suspended," T.J. growled.

The words that came out of his father's mouth expressing his rage, murderous rage, said everything that T.J. had wanted to say in Captain Smith's office. T.J. pressed the phone to his ear, enjoying this moment. His dad understood the injustice being done to him. Those black boys don't matter; he was just teaching them to stay in their place. He wasn't concerned about the investigation; his rage stemmed from another black boy who had thought he was an equal, not staying in his place. "Well, Son, I guess our plans for Weston will have to be moved up. I just got off the phone with your cousin Roy. He's got more information on that reward money, and he thinks he has seen that woman they're looking for. Maybe we can kill two birds with one stone. Come on by the house. We got some work to do."

"Okay, Dad, I'm on my way."

Chapter 12

Kevin woke suddenly from the nightmare that had haunted him for the majority of his life. He could still hear his mom's screams, then nothing. He listened as his breathing slowed, and then sitting up in his bed, he prayed as he always did. He sat for a long time, thinking about his nightmare, wondering why it still haunted him. He prayed again, "Father, I know you were with my parents that night, and I know that they are in heaven with you even now. Why am I still plagued by that night? I think I saw something, but I don't know what it was. I've tried to look into it, but I haven't been able to find anything. I really want to get closure on what happened that night. Please show me how to do that. Thank you, Father, in Jesus name, amen." As Kevin settled down to go back to sleep, Sam Alexander's name came to his mind. He had thought about Sam a couple of times before but always brushed it off. Tonight he asked out loud, "Do I need to talk to Sam about the accident, Father?"

He felt peace wash over him and accepted that as his answer. He made a mental note to stop by and visit Sam at the Table to help out and spend some time with him.

Kevin considered Sam, a close friend of the family. He was what most people would call a giant, 6'5" tall with broad shoulders; he looked like a lumberjack. He had dark brown, curly hair, and blue eyes, his skin was tan from years of working and living outdoors. Grams had met him years ago and adopted him as one of her many sons. Kevin didn't know much about Sam, just that he served in the military, and that when he first came to Resting Place, he was homeless. Kevin had met him after he started working at the soup kitchen. A few years ago Sam had accepted the manager position. When Grams gave a party to celebrate his promotion, Kevin remembered how surprised and humbled Sam was. He never really talked about himself, but he was always around to help Grams. Kevin could see that Sam was just as much a part of his family as J.P. and Trace were, and he knew that Sam loved Grams without question. She only had one biological child, Kevin's mom. God had given her hundreds of children to love, and Sam was one of them. As Kevin drifted off to sleep, he smiled and reminded himself to take Sam some of Grams' pineapple coconut cake.

≈≈≈

T.J. and Timothy Muller sat at a table in the back of McKinney Bar and Grill waiting for Roy Grimes. T.J. was agitated; ever since his suspension, he felt off-kilter, out of sorts. Those feelings only added fuel to his anger towards Kevin Weston. His hatred knew no bounds when it came to Kevin; he had never liked him. T.J. thought Kevin should be kept in his place, and with his dad's help, he would see to it. "Where is Roy?" Timothy Muller grunted, "That boy is always late. If we didn't need him to pull this off, I wouldn't even bother with him."

"There he is," T.J. said, waving Roy over to the table. Together the three men discussed how they would exchange information on where to locate this Monica woman. Roy explained while boasting about his conversation with a guy he had met in a bar a few towns over. The guy worked for some big-time drug lord who wanted to find this woman so badly that he would pay a hundred grand for information to get to her. Roy said that the exchange would happen on Friday night near the old farmhouse by the railroad tracks near the end of town. The deal was that half the money would be paid for the information and the other half when they located the woman. They agreed to split the reward three ways, and T.J. and Roy would meet the guy on Friday night. All three men were satisfied with the plan, feeling smug about their good fortune. They ordered another round of drinks and leaned back, talking about old times.

T.J. had been thinking about resigning ever since he was put on suspension. He felt things were changing, and this would be a time to leave the force. Finishing up his drink, he made up his mind that he would hand in his resignation paperwork on Friday. He had a really nice nest egg set aside, and with this additional money and Weston out of his way, he could leave Resting Place, move a few towns away, and maybe start a security business. T.J. believed this investigation was just a routine thing, and even with that black kid showing up, they would not be able to do anything to him. No one in their right mind would remove him for roughing up a few blacks, and after Friday it wouldn't be an issue because he would be gone. Timothy let out a loud belch and said, "I know where the house is. T.J., didn't you tell me that Weston goes out there a lot?"

"Yeah, he goes out there quite a bit, but I'm not sure why " T.J. replied.

Roy jumped in, "Yeah, he was out there the night I tried to get Janie."

Timothy continued with his story, "Thomas and I were best friends and partners until he turned scared, yellow, about how they took care of Kevin Weston Sr. Tom started getting paranoid and drinking all the time to cope. He was going to be put off the force for being unfit for duty. He kept saying he wanted to stop the voices in his head; darn fool ran his truck into a tree and killed himself." Shaking his head at the memory, Timothy continued, "We used to ride out there when he was dating Brandy. The house is pretty isolated, and a lot of people don't know how to get out there, but I do." He grinned. "Now we just need to make sure Weston is with this Monica woman when the guy gets there. With a little help from T.J. and me, we'll make sure that Weston dies in the line of duty." At the end of the day, Weston would be out of the picture, they would be a lot richer, and T.J. could move on. Yes, it was time to move on.

Chapter 13

Kevin and Trace sat at a table by the window at Emma's Diner; a small family-owned restaurant near Resting Place High School. Emma, the owner, offered police discounts to provide a police presence for the youth in the community. Kevin, Trace and a few other officers has provided mentoring services for the high schoolers in the community as a result of Emma's discounts.

"Trace, do you have any plans for Thursday night?" Kevin asked.

"No, what's up?"

"Grams is having a get-together around six. I'm taking Lilly to meet the family; so far everybody's going to be there."

"So, this is getting pretty serious?" Trace replied with a smile.

"I've wasted so much time over the last two years. Now, since we've been seeing each other, I can't imagine living my life without her. I want her to get to know the rest of my family; she already knows you and Tate."

Trace grinned, "So I'm counted as family?"

"Closer than a brother," Kevin responded with a serious look, then smiled and said, "Besides, Grams would box my ears if I didn't make sure you were there."

"Okay, I'll be there."

"Oh, bring a change of clothes; we're going to play some basketball."

"Great! It's been a little while since we've played. What time should I be over?" Trace asked as he paid for his food.

"The rest of the response team will be there around five. I'm picking up Lilly at four; if you like you can meet us at Safe Haven and follow us to Grams'. I know Maggie will be doing some counseling, so maybe she can ride with you." Kevin winked at Trace.

Trace smiled and said, "Thanks, Kevin."

"Anytime, Cowboy."

≈≈≈

Lilly was beyond nervous, she had changed outfits three times and still felt like nothing was right. She was meeting Kevin's family; she could hardly believe that he wanted her to be around his family. She had talked with him the previous night before he went home. Their nightly phone calls had turned into Kevin stopping by on the way home, then talking on the phone as he drove home and praying before saying goodnight. A few weeks ago, Lilly dreaded that time of night; now she looked forward to it and was even excited about it since it included Kevin Weston. At first, she was happy about meeting his family, but then concern crept in. She had asked over and over if he was sure he wanted her to meet his family. "That's a big deal, Kevin; they may think that we're getting serious if you take me home to meet them." Lilly had cautioned.

"I know, and I am getting serious, Lilly. I don't want a casual relationship with you." Reaching out and cupping her chin, he had continued, "You mean far too much to me." His voice had become deeper as he whispered, "I want you to be a part of my life. I know we haven't been dating very long, but I want you to understand that I want a lifetime with you, Lilly."

Lilly had just stared, her heart so full of love for Kevin. "For real?"

Kevin had leaned in and kissed the scar on her face. "Yes, for real." Moving to her lips, he had kissed her, trying to convey how much he loved her. Pulling away a little breathless, he repeated, "Really Lilly, I want a lifetime with you."

Knees weak, Lilly whispered, "Okay."

As he turned to leave, Lilly's heart was so full she whispered, "I love you."

Kevin stopped in his tracks, turned around, and looked deeply into her eyes. "I love you, too, Lilly." Walking back to her, he gave her a gentle kiss and held her tight before saying good night.

The doorbell brought Lilly out of her daze; she grabbed her first choice, a peach-colored sundress with a flower print. She told herself that the late June heat and humidity the past few days helped her choose the sundress. Tossing her sneakers, a tee shirt, and sweatpants in her shoulder bag, she hurried out of her room to meet Kevin.

Without looking, Kevin knew the moment Lilly walked into the living room. He could feel her presence; all his senses were aware of her nearness. He knew his brother and sister shared a unique bond because they were twins, but the bond that was forming between Lilly and himself was like nothing he had ever experienced. They could talk for hours. Lilly was a chatterbox. He hadn't expected to enjoy so much talking, but he did. He hung on to her every word. Kevin found that Lilly didn't just talk about random topics that came to mind. Her conversations were about things that were important to her—her brother, the courses she took in college, what she wanted to do with her counseling degree, and her faith. Kevin drank in her words. The sound of her voice and her facial expressions made him feel like a man in the desert finally getting water. He loved Lilly. He had gone home the previous night after their amazing kiss and her sweet voice telling him that she loved him. He could hardly contain the emotions those words stirred in him. It took all his willpower not to fall on his knee and ask Lilly then and there to marry him. Instead, he settled for receiving that incredible kiss and assuring her of his love.

Today she would meet his family, the people he loved most. He hadn't made a big deal out of this get-together, but the truth of the matter was that it was a huge deal for him. He had never brought anyone home to Grams, not even Susie. He had thought about taking Susie home, but other things had always taken priority. Looking back, he realized Susie was right; he loved his job more than her. Now with Lilly, he couldn't wait until his shift ended so he could go see her. Lilly was on his mind all day, and he had to force himself to focus on work. He knew in his heart that Lilly was the one for him. He felt different around her. She made him feel as if he could do anything. She was in his corner; she made him feel special. Kevin had never known these feelings. He had never been in love before now.

"Hi, Kevin," Lilly said with that heart-stopping smile of hers.

"Hi, Lilly. You ready to go?" Kevin smiled as they gazed at each other.

"Hey, Lilly." Trace said, breaking Kevin and Lilly's silent communication.

Maggie walked into the living room, greeting the group, "Hi, everybody. Are we ready?"

"Yeah," Trace cleared his throat. "Kevin and Lilly are riding in his truck. You want to ride with me?" Trace asked Maggie. He was trying to sound casual, but he was nervous about asking her. He had taken Kevin and Grams' advice about how to approach Maggie. He just hoped God would bless him with her friendship and give them time to get to know each other because he felt in his heart of hearts that she was the one.

Trace didn't believe in love at first sight until his eyes fell on that red-haired fireball named Maggie Hart at one of the First Response team meetings. She was laughing with Kevin about something, and Trace was floored by how her laughter affected him. He felt like he lost a tiny part of his heart to her that day, and over the past few years, he had continued to lose parts of his heart to her. The bad news was that Maggie had never so much as looked at Trace as a friend. While he was hopelessly in love with her, she didn't even like him. Trace was at a loss as to what to do.

The previous night after Bible Study, Trace had offered to take Grams home, desperate to talk about what was weighing on his heart. Two cups of coffee and several challenging questions later, Trace had gained the direction he needed. Gram had listened as he poured out his heart about the feelings he had for Maggie. He had talked about the frustration of her not even acknowledging him as a friend, and how hopeless the whole thing seemed. Grams had asked him one question, "What has God told you, Trace?"

Trace had let out a breath, "He gives the Scripture of love never fails. Every time I pray about it I get that Scripture. I don't know what to do, Grams." He had dropped his face in his hands, feeling hopeless about what else he could do or say.

Then Grams had asked, "Trace, are you willing to sacrifice the love you have for Maggie to become the friend she needs right now? I believe Kevin is right, I think Maggie does care for you, but she has a lot of hurt to sort through. Right now she needs a friend to walk with her. Are you willing to be that friend?"

"I think, I am. I want to be. Grams, can we pray about it?"

After praying, Trace had given Grams a hug and a kiss on the cheek, whispering in her ear, "Thanks, Grams, I love you."

"I love you too, child."

Driving home, Trace had decided to spend the rest of the night seeking God about how to be a friend to Maggie, expecting nothing in return. In the wee hours of the morning, he had risen from his knees and thanked God for the peace and guidance he received.

Maggie noticed how Kevin and Lilly were looking at each other. She had heard that they were dating, and she was happy for them, realizing they probably didn't need any company on the ride to Grams' house. However, she wasn't sure about riding with Trace. Maggie wasn't comfortable with the way Trace made her feel. He could make her stomach do flip-flops without saying a word. He caused her face to heat up with a smile, and he was a little flirtatious. She didn't know how to deal with it. He was a nice guy, and she liked him, but she didn't want to like him too much, so she kept her distance. She scolded herself about over-thinking the whole thing. *It's just a ride to Grams; get a grip, girl.* "Okay, thanks, let me get my bag." Smiling, she went to get her gym bag.

Trace whispered, "Thank you, Father." He smiled at Kevin and told him they could leave and he would meet them at Grams' house with Maggie.

Chapter 14

The first thing Lilly noticed when she walked into Grams' house was the feeling of home. She couldn't think of a better description. She felt as if she had just come home. Then she saw Grams–petite and, slim, her long, black hair with a few strands of gray, pulled back in a loose ponytail and the most amazing, hazel eyes. She had to be in her late sixties or early seventies, yet she looked and carried herself like a much younger woman.

She walked up to Lilly and without a word, enfolded her into a big hug; Lilly hugged her back, loving the feel of this woman's embrace. Ending the hug Grams smiled with tears in her eyes she said, "Lilly, welcome to our home. I'm so glad to meet you."

Overwhelmed by the instant affection she felt for Grams, Lilly responded, "Thank you for having me, Mrs. Rose."

"Lilly, please call me Grams." Grams gave her another hug and then hugged Kevin. "Why don't you head out back where the rest of the kids are out there? Oh, where's Trace?"

Kevin smiled, "He should be here in a few minutes, he was waiting for Maggie." Grams smiled and scooted them out of the back door.

Lilly was enjoying herself; Kevin's family was so nice to her. Sidney gave her a big hug and thanked her for making her brother smile. Stephanie, Marcus' fiancée, welcomed her to the family and told her that anytime she needed to talk or shop to just let her know. Grams enlisted Lilly's help in the kitchen and shared stories about Kevin; some made Lilly laugh, and others made her heart swell even more with love for him.

Kevin walked over to Lilly after dinner and asked, "Can we take a walk before someone else steals you away from me?"

As they walked out the back door, Kevin pulled her off to the side of the house and kissed her, while holding her face in his hands. Sighing, he said, "I needed that." Stroking her cheek, he complained, "I knew my family would love you, but I didn't plan on them taking you away from me. I haven't seen you all night."

Lilly couldn't stop the giggle that escaped as she watched him pout about not spending time with her. Was this man real? "Kevin, I love your family, and I'm having such a good time. Thank you for bringing me." Lilly reached up and kissed him softly on the lips.

Kevin smiled, looking into her eyes and whispering, "Lilly you are so incredibly beautiful. I love you." Lilly dropped her head without responding. Kevin gently lifted her face, asking, "Hey, what's wrong?"

"Kevin, I'm too scarred to be beautiful. You don't have to say it."

"No, Lilly you are the most beautiful woman I've ever seen. These scars…" Kevin paused stroking her cheek, "are visible signs of your love for Rico. I remember your first night here; I was watching you sleep, asking myself what would it feel like to be loved like that? You would risk everything, even your life for Rico. Lilly, that's real love, Rico would be so proud of you; I know I am." Leaning in, he kissed her again. Pulling back, Kevin looked into her eyes and repeated his words in a soft whisper, "You are the most beautiful, amazing woman I have ever known."

Lilly smiled with tears in her eyes and said, "Thank you."

Kevin pulled her into his arms and held her. Closing her eyes and breathing in a contented sigh, Lilly realized that Kevin made her feel beautiful.

≈≈≈

Hector settled back in the seat of a private jet, courtesy of his older brother, waiting for takeoff. The blonde wig, blue contacts, and slimmer body gave him a whole new look. He had lost weight and buffed up while in prison. He never liked exercising but found that staying in shape was a part of survival. His new identity, Simon Smart, was delivered to him the previous night at the hotel with a package of information to study and memorize. Hector loved the name, Simon Smart and chuckled when he was told it belonged to a real person. He felt the name was very appropriate since he had outsmarted the prison guards and the police. Now he was on his way to pay a visit to sweet, innocent Monica. It was a stroke of luck that Little Joe, one of Hector's guys stumbled on some information that Monica was somewhere in Maryland. He would meet with Little Joe as soon as the plane landed. Hector made up his mind to reward Little Joe; he would tell him that he could have the reward money if he got rid of the guy and cleaned up the mess. He took a deep breath and sighed. He was free, and Monica would pay for setting him up. Smiling, he patted the carry-on filled with money on the seat next to him.

As the pilot's voice came through the speaker, preparing for takeoff, Hector's phone rang. Smiling, he answered, "Brother, how are you?"

Hector's brother, Roberto's voice, boomed through the phone, "Hector, we had to pull a lot of strings and take out a few people to get you free. Now, what is this I hear about you going to Maryland? Leave that woman for your boys to take care of. It's too risky for you."

"No, she didn't betray my boys, she betrayed me. You know me, Roberto; I'll kill her, just like her little brother. This is personal. I'll handle it."

"Well, if you must do this, be careful. I need the jet back tonight. I'm flying out in the morning to meet some associates about recruiting in a new market in Montana."

"No problem, I should be done with this by midnight. I'll see you in the morning."

≈≈≈

Kevin and Lilly walked hand and hand back into the house smiling. Kevin noticed Sam Alexander talking with Grams and decided to speak with him before taking Lilly home. Leaning down, he whispered in Lilly's ear, "Hey, I want to see Sam before we leave. It shouldn't take long."

"No problem. Stephanie and Maggie want to set up a girl's night out; I'll be over with them when you're ready."

Kevin reached over and caressed her cheek, then walked over to Sam. Kevin extended his hand and said, "Hi, Mr. Sam, how are you tonight?"

Sam replied, "I 'm doing well and glad you came over. I was hoping to speak with you this Saturday, but if you have a few minutes, we could talk now."

Kevin answered, "I wanted to chat with you, too. I've been praying about my parents and the accident, and God keeps giving me your name."

Sam nodded, "I think I can help you with that, young Kevin."

Kevin shook his head at the name, "young Kevin." Where had he heard that name?

Ben Rayns walked over with his phone at his ear. "Kevin, we need to talk. Get everybody together and meet me in the backyard."

Hearing the concern in Uncle Ben's voice, Kevin asked, "What's happened?"

Ben leaned closer and said, "It's about Hector Ramos. He's still alive."

Kevin stared at Uncle Ben and then searched the room until he located Lilly talking with Sidney. "We'll meet you in the backyard."

Five minutes later the Response Team was assembled in the yard, seated at the picnic table by a big oak tree away from the house. Trace asked, "What's going on, Ben? Kevin says Hector is still alive."

Ben replied, "I knew it was too easy. It seems that the guy that was beaten to death wasn't Hector. The coroner's report was delayed due to staff shortages. It just came back today. The body was identified as Juan Cortez, who was supposed to have been released the day before Hector's death."

Kevin asked, "So where is he? Do we have any idea if he knows where Lilly is? What can we do to keep her safe?" Kevin realized he was beginning to sound like Lilly with his rapid-fire questions. Taking a deep, calming breath, he resisted asking another question and waited for Uncle Ben to answer.

"We don't know where he is, and we're going to assume that he does know where Lilly is. We'll relocate her tonight. I think we're still ahead of this, but I know there's a leak at the prison; Hector had help getting out of that facility. He's pretty powerful and has a long reach, and I'm concerned about just how far it goes. As of right now, we're going off the grid. Not a word to anyone else. We want to catch Hector, and the best way to do that is to let him come to us. Kevin, you, Trace and Maggie take Lilly to my cabin, and stay out of sight." Looking at Brandy, Ben asked, "Are there any residents at Safe Haven right now?"

"No, the last one left this morning."

"Good." Turning to Tate, Ben continued, "Tate, you and Brandy will work with a few handpicked officers and me, at Safe Haven. We only have a very small window of time; let's make the best of it." Looking at Kevin, he said, "I want you guys on the road in the next half hour."

Twenty-five minutes later, two SUVs left Grams' house, heading for the interstate. Ben was making some phone calls when Sam

Alexander walked into Grams' study; Ben gave him a questioning look. "What can I do for you, Sam?"

Sending up a silent prayer, Sam said, "I need to talk with 'Jayhawk.'"

Ben was surprised to hear his military code name. Thinking fast, he asked, "Who needs to talk to Jayhawk?"

"Ghost needs to talk with him."

Ben recognized the name and motioned for Sam to close the door before saying anything else.

Chapter 15

L illy was in a state of shock. How could Hector be alive and free? How did he escape? Fear began to overtake her as she tried to process the news. One minute she was planning a night out with Sidney, Stephanie, and Maggie; the next moment she was being handed a bag of clothes and food and rushed out the door. Looking over at Kevin, she wondered, *what's next*

Kevin sensing her stress, placed his hand over hers and said, "I know this was sudden. This move is a precaution to keep you safe." He was kind but professional and detached, very different from the Kevin she had spent time with just a few hours ago. Looking at him she replied, "Okay."

Way to go, Kevin thought to himself. She's scared and trying to hold it together, and I'm treating her like a job, an assignment. At that moment he realized that he was not in control and that ultimately he couldn't keep Lilly safe. He had to trust God to keep them both. Taking a deep breath, he said, "Lilly, honey, I'm sorry. I know this is a lot to take in and I haven't been much help to you since we told you all this at the house. It's just... it's just that I love you so much and I don't know what I would do without you in my life. I've been praying, and I know I need to trust that God will protect you. Can we pray about this and ask Him to keep all of us safe?"

"Oh Kevin, I thought you had changed your mind about us, about me. I thought you felt like I was too much trouble."

"No, Lilly, I'm going to marry you. I want that lifetime that we talked about."

Lilly gave him one of those heart-stopping smiles and said, "I want that, too."

"Let's pray." Kevin's baritone voice lifted his concerns to the Lord, asking for wisdom in keeping Lilly safe; praying protection over their group; commanding every attack of the enemy to be canceled, and God's divine guidance, protection and favor for them. He prayed for Trace and Maggie and then for his brother Tate and his Uncle Ben. After the prayer, Lilly felt peace flow over her, and when she looked at Kevin, she couldn't control the big smile that lit up her face. She felt safe in a way she had never experienced. She knew God loved her, and that she could trust Him to keep them safe. Lilly leaned over to Kevin, kissed his cheek and asked, "So, where will you take me for our next date?"

Seeing the joy on her face, Kevin laughed. He loved this woman with all his heart, and their next date might just be the right time to ask her to marry him. He leaned over and said, "It's a surprise." He grinned as Lilly pouted about his answer. This woman was absolutely adorable. He prayed a silent prayer of thanksgiving for blessing him with Lilly.

≈≈≈

Maggie just couldn't get herself together, she had been riding with Trace for almost two hours, and her stomach was still doing flip-flops. Trace's GMC Yukon was the same size as Kevin's; the only difference was that Trace's was black. It was a big truck, but it felt like a tiny closet. She was aware of so many things about him. The scent of his cologne was a fresh, clean smell that teased her nose. She couldn't ignore the sound of his rich, smooth, baritone voice as he sang along with the radio or the concern in his voice when he asked if she was okay as if he really cared. This man was a puzzle to her, and she felt at a disadvantage whenever she was in close proximity of him. Unfortunately, she couldn't do anything about it. She closed her eyes and silently prayed for God to make a way of escape from all the emotions Trace was stirring within her. As she finished, she heard a still, quiet voice whispering to her soul. *You can trust him, daughter. He won't hurt you.* She knew the voice of the Lord, and she recognized what she had just heard was Him. Maggie turned and looked at Trace for so long he turned and said, "What? Is something wrong?"

"No, I was just thinking." She smiled.

"What were you thinking about, if you don't mind sharing?"

Thinking fast, Maggie answered, "About God and how His will doesn't always make sense." She had used that topic about God many times to end unwanted conversations with guys trying to hit on her. It was her "go to" subject, and it had served her well over the years.

Trace pondered her words, and then responded, "I can say amen to that. It can be so frustrating when we think everything is going according to plan, and God throws a monkey wrench in the middle of it."

"Yeah, exactly. You think everything is set, and you're happy with everything one minute, and the next you're trying to get your balance because you just got thrown a curve ball."

Trace and Maggie entered into a long, engaging conversation about God's perfect will and how helpless they were at getting it right on their own. When they pulled up at Ben Rayns' cabin, Trace said, "Thank you for sharing with me. I really enjoyed talking with you."

Maggie responded, teasing, "Thank you. I didn't know you were into God like that."

Trace responded, "Hey, I'm a preacher's kid; I have learned a little bit. To be honest, I love the Lord; I always have. I just don't have a lot of people around to share it with, except Kevin."

"Well, maybe we can talk again sometime." Maggie almost put her hand over her mouth to shut herself up. *What was she doing? Inviting conversation with Trace Kenton?*

Trace smiled, "I'd like that. Okay, let's check the house out and get them inside."

≈≈≈

Ben and Tate sat drinking coffee at 4:00 a.m. Friday morning waiting for Officer Rodriguez to arrive. Officer Maria Rodriguez had volunteered to be a decoy for Lilly. From a distance, she could easily pass for Lilly. They had worked most of the night, putting things in place to ensure they would get enough evidence to build an ironclad case against Hector. They had even placed some additional high powered surveillance cameras around the property. The cameras were strategically located to capture all approachable angles in both front and back of the property. Tate and Ben studied the screen as a 1965 cannonball red Mustang drove up to the house. Tate whistled and said, "Nice car!" He moved closer to the monitor to get a better look at the vehicle. As a young child, he had loved the old "muscle" cars of the past. After returning from the military, Tate had found restoring the old cars therapeutic. Often when he woke from nightmares, working on an old car and praying calmed him. He could see several things on the Mustang that could easily be fixed to bring it to its full level of former glory. Lost in his thoughts, Tate didn't notice Maria Rodriguez get out of the car and enter the building. The chimes of the doorbell drew him from his daydreaming.

Tate followed Uncle Ben to the front door. As Maria walked in and introduced herself to Ben,

Tate found himself thinking, *Wow, the five-foot, no inches woman seems to brighten the room.* Her curly brown hair was pulled back into a long ponytail that barely held all the curls. Officer Rodriguez wore a pink tee shirt and straight-legged blue jeans. The words "casual beauty" came to his mind. Refocusing, he heard Ben address Maria.

"Officer Rodriguez, thank you for coming on such short notice." Ben's voice held his appreciation of her assistance. "I understand that you're currently on vacation with your family. How are your parents? It's been a while since I've touched base with them."

"They're both doing well, and wanted me to remind you that you owe them a visit," Maria replied with a smile. "Dad said to give him a call later this week to make plans for a visit."

"I 'll do that; I'll have some free time after this case." Ben then turned to Tate and said, "Lt. Rodriguez, I want to introduce you to Dr. Tate Weston. I believe you know his brother Lt. Kevin Weston."

Maria replied, "Yes, I've worked a few cases with Lt. Weston." Smiling, she extended her hand to Tate.

Their hands made contact at the same time their eyes met, and the combination rocked Tate. He felt as if the earth moved. What is this? Tate wondered as he had never had this kind of reaction to any female, ever. *Who was this woman, and why did he react so strongly?* Tate concluded that he had to process these feelings as soon as he was alone. He would be working closely with Lt. Rodriguez and didn't need any distractions. Clearing his throat, Tate said, "Good morning, Lt. Rodriguez. It's nice to meet you."

Maria was trying desperately to clear her head. *Where did this guy come from?* She thought she was immune to the attraction of handsome men. She had always heard her girlfriends talk about sparks and their hearts beating out of their chests, but she had never experienced anything like that, not even the flicker of a spark or a thump-thump of a heartbeat. So, why was her heart beating so loudly she knew everyone could hear it? And why was her hand, which Tate was still holding, tingling all the way up her arm? "It's nice to meet you as well, Dr. Weston." Maria managed as she eased her hand out of his. She wanted to rub it down the side of her jeans, to stop the tingling but didn't want to show how much she was affected. Instead, she settled for putting her hands in her pants pockets.

Ben Rayns smiled as he noticed what happened between Tate and Maria. At that moment he began a silent prayer for God to prepare Tate's heart for the mate that He would send or had already sent.

"Maria, we'll be working pretty closely here, so I think we can be informal since there are only four of us in the house. Brandy Hart is in the kitchen working on some breakfast. We have surveillance cameras and ten men posted around the property. Our role is to make this place appear as normal. We requested you because of your similarities to our witness. You'll follow her routine today and hopefully draw Hector out." Ben handed Maria a sheet of paper, and continued, "We've compiled a list of the daily activities of our witness. Tate will be with you today, He's not a police officer, but he is a highly skilled member of our response team, and he can pretty much handle anything that may come your way, not that you couldn't take care of yourself. However, today you are Lilly Collin, so we don't want to blow your cover." Ben said with a smile, knowing that he just annoyed Maria.

Brandy walked in the office, saying, "I thought I heard the doorbell. Hi, you must be Maria?" Extending her hand, she said, "Hi, I'm Brandy Hart. It's good to meet you."

Maria responded, "Hi, Ms. Hart. It is good to meet you as well." she sniffed the air before asking, "Are those cinnamon rolls I smell?"

Grinning, Brandy replied, "Yes, they are. Ben said he wanted to appear as normal as possible, so I felt like making some with breakfast this morning. I tend to cook when I have a lot on my mind. Anyway, the rolls should be ready now, so let's eat."

Chapter 16

Hector sat in the black SUV waiting for information that would get him to Monica that night. He was annoyed with his brother for putting him on a time limit. He wanted to take his time with Monica, to ensure that she paid to his satisfaction for her betrayal. His brother's morning appointment caused him to rush his plans. He would have to make due; the results would be the same. Monica would pay, and that would have to be enough.

"Where is this guy with my information?" Hector barked after waiting for 10 minutes. He decided to go over the plan one more time, having learned over the years that repeating what he wanted done usually worked well, especially right before a job. He had been on the receiving end of leaders who didn't want to repeat their instructions, and they paid high prices for their arrogance. "Okay, let's go over the plan again. When he comes, we'll get the details; I'll hand over the money and get into the car. You'll tell him to check the case, and while he's looking at the money, shoot him. I want this to be quick and easy. We're on a tight schedule." Hector looked Little Joe in the eyes to convey his point.

"I understand, Boss, quick and easy."

As they finished talking, a dark blue Ford F-150 truck drove up with two men in it. Hector wasn't expecting two; already his plans were changing. He whispered the question under his breath, "Can you kill them both?"

"Yeah, sure, Boss. I can do that."

Smiling, Hector addressed the men, "Do you have my information?"

T.J. Muller assessed the situation. He had already checked out the area earlier that day and had done his research on Monica Sanchez. He knew the guy he was talking to was Hector Ramos and realized that if they didn't play the cards right, they would not leave this exchange alive. Hector couldn't afford to have any witnesses, so T.J. had brought a little extra insurance.

T.J. smiled back at Hector before answering, "Sure do."

Hector mumbled under his breath, not liking the cocky answer. "Well, give it to me." Hector nodded to Little Joe to move toward T.J.

"Hold it right there, Spick."

Hector's rage was instant as he yelled, "What did you call me?" He reached for his gun.

Little red dots starting dancing on Hector's and Little Joe's chests. Guns were trained on them, and Hector realized he had walked into a trap. His anger only amused T.J., who hated Hispanics almost as much as he hated blacks. It felt good to get the upper hand and take what he wanted. Laughing, he said, "Drop your guns. Now let's do business, boys. My partner and I want full payment for the information we have, and since we seem to have the advantage here, we'll just take all your money. You just drop the bag and kick it over here." When the bag was a safe distance away from Hector and Little Joe, T.J. continued, "Now, empty your pockets." As they complied, T.J. told Roy check out the car, and take only cash.

Satisfied that they had gotten what they wanted, T.J. held up a piece of white paper saying, "Here is your information—there's the address and some directions. My partner and I will be leaving now, but our insurance will stick around for a few more minutes just to make sure we aren't followed. I suggest you handle your business and leave our town."

Hector stood paralyzed by the red dot while that man took all their money and drove away. The longest 10 minutes of Hector's life passed before the red dot disappeared. Breathing deeply he walked over and picked up the paper. Hector clutched it in his hand, and without saying a word, got in the truck and drove away.

Once they were on the main highway, Little Joe asked, "Where to now, Boss?"

Hector took a couple of deep breaths, fighting to control the anger that man had stirred up in him. He had realized as a young man that angry men made mistakes; he had used that to his advantage many times. He also realized that time was running out. He had to get rid of Monica tonight. He hated that nothing had gone his way so far. He would have preferred to leave and come back for Monica after getting a clear head. He handed Little Joe the paper and said, "One thing at a time. First, we take care of Monica, and then we take care of those two dogs who took our money."

≈≈≈

T.J. Muller was on the top of the world. He felt great; outsmarting Hector Ramos and now getting rid of Weston gave him great joy. He hadn't felt that good in a long time. His excitement grew as the night wore on. That night he would get rid of the constant thorn in his side. Grinning, he could hardly contain his feelings. Pulling out his phone, he dialed his dad's number. "Hey, Dad."

"How did it go, Son?"

T.J. could hear the pride in his father's voice. "Like a charm. You sure called it right, Dad. They thought we were hicks they could use and get rid of; they didn't even see it coming. You should've seen their faces when they found out we had them. And we took all their money. Hector sure was mad, but we had him dead to rights, and he couldn't do a thing about it."

"Did you give them the information about that girl?"

"Sure did. I told them to handle their business, and get out of town." T.J. high fived Roy as he told his dad how they walked away, leaving Hector and his man frozen in place. It was time to leave Resting Place; Hector was not going to just walk away. After tonight T.J.

would disappear for a while until things calmed down. Content with his plans, he said, "We're on the way to pick you up and finish our work for the night."

Chapter 17

At 4:30 p.m. Trace became restless. Kevin watched him pace back and forth every few minutes. Trace checked the window, stared into the distance, then paced some more. After thirty minutes of this, Kevin walked over to him and asked, "What's going on, Cowboy?"

"I don't know; I'm just on high alert." Trace whispered.

Kevin gave him a slight nod and replied, "Holy Spirit alert? What are you getting?"

"Pray, that's all I'm getting. I don't know what's going on back home, but I really think we need to stay in prayer for them."

Kevin thought about Tate, Uncle Ben, Maggie and Maria at Safe Haven and how much they would be facing that night. Then he asked, "How about an all-nighter, fasting and praying?"

Trace smiled and replied, "As Grams would say, our prayer can go where we cannot."

Kevin nodded and said, "I'll go get the girls and our Bibles, and we can get started."

Twenty minutes later they were all in the rustic living room lifting their voices in prayer.

At 7:00 p.m. Kevin's phone rang. Lilly was praying. Not wanting to distract her, he stepped out of the room. In the kitchen, he saw Captain Smith's number on his phone and answered, "Hello."

The captain's bass voice came on the line, "Kevin, we have some disturbing news. I don't know where you are, but you need to get back here. One of our officers pulled over Officer Phil Major tonight; he was driving an unmarked car with a tail light out. Officer Travis Black probably wouldn't have stopped him if he had known it was Phil. Travis stated Major was really nervous when he pulled him over, which caused him to look into the car. He found a sniper rifle in his back seat. Travis knew Major was on suspension and called it in. We made him come in for questioning. We told him that in light of the suspension and the investigation, we would detain him until Internal Affairs meets next week. He started complaining that T.J. said the investigation was a routine thing, no big deal. I told him that the investigation would determine if he remains on the force and that he could be facing criminal charges. Once he understood how much trouble he was in, he starting asking for a deal to break a big case. It took a while to get Internal Affairs to agree. Major told us that T.J. met with Hector Ramos tonight and gave him the location of the safe house. He also said that he overheard T.J. and his dad making plans to go to the safe house to get rid of Weston. I know Marshal Rayns is expecting Hector, but if T.J. is with him, they'll need help. I would like this to end without bloodshed if possible."

"Okay, Captain, I'll brief Trace then head back."

Everyone looked up when Kevin walked back into the room. Trace asked what the call was about. Kevin told them about Hector and T.J. and started to say that he had to head back. Before he could finish, Trace shook his head and said, "No, we don't go into unstable situations alone." Kevin knew that rule, which had allowed them to walk away from many bad situations. The look Trace gave him told Kevin that he was not going alone.

Lilly put her hand on Kevin's arm. "Kevin, I know you want me safe, but I've been trained to protect myself and the women at Safe Haven. And once this is over with Hector, I'll be joining the Response Team. There's no reason for us to stay here when they need our help. If it would make you feel better, I can stay locked in one of the rooms in the basement with Maggie. I have a feeling Ben will need all of you.

Kevin looked at Maggie, who said, "Mom's there, Kevin. It's your call, but I want to help and make sure she's okay."

Kevin sent up a silent prayer for wisdom. Closing his eyes, he waited. *Lord, please show me what to do; these are all the people I love.* A calm came over him as the thought came to him, *Uncle Ben needs you. Trust me with the rest.* Opening his eyes, he looked from Lilly to Trace and said, "Okay, let's get on the road."

Twenty minutes later the two SUVs headed back to Safe Haven, with Kevin and Trace talking on their cell phones, going over plans on how to get in the house undetected. Listening to the sound of Kevin's voice, Lilly drifted to sleep.

Kevin decided to let her rest, he would fill her in later about the trail, and he had to give her the extra gun he had in the lock box under his seat. He prayed for wisdom and protection for the team and Lilly, that no lives would be lost and that Lilly's nightmares would finally be over. The more he prayed, the more things God reminded him to pray about. Two and a half hours later, he thanked God for the peace he received and praised God that He would have the victory tonight. Reaching over, he squeezed Lilly's hand, asking, "You okay?"

Lilly sat up, wiping sleep out of her eyes, something Kevin was sure he could get used to seeing. "I'm sorry, what did you say?"

Kevin smiled, "Are you okay?"

Lilly thought about it and decided that she would hold nothing back from Kevin. She didn't know what would happen with Hector and T.J., but she did know she had the present moment with Kevin, and she wanted him to know what he meant to her. "I'm terrified, but I couldn't stay behind. I wanted to be with you. When I was training, I wanted to learn everything I could to protect myself and the women at Safe Haven, but also to help the team. I've prayed about it, and even though I'm scared, I know I'm doing the right thing. And..." her voice dropped to a whisper, "I love you too much to stay behind." Lilly hung her head, uneasy about revealing her love for him; it was so new to her.

Kevin's heart nearly exploded with love at her words. Without saying a word he put on his right signal light and pulled over on the shoulder of the road. Kevin texted Trace that he needed a minute to talk with Lilly. Putting his phone in his shirt pocket, he reached over and gathered her in his arms and said, "I love you so much! I don't know what I did to deserve you, but I promise I'll spend the rest of my life loving you, Lilly." He pulled her close, kissing her with all the love he held in his heart for her. Pulling away and breathing deeply, he continued, "I want forever with you. I believe God will give us forever. So let's take care of the past so that we can get on with our future."

Lilly's heart was so full; she had the biggest smile on her face, and she couldn't hold the incredible joy she felt inside. Looking into Kevin's eyes and seeing his love for her gave her the boldness to lean in and kiss him, a slow, lingering kiss that took his breath away.

A tapping sound invaded Kevin's mind, as he released Lilly and opened his eyes; he realized someone was tapping on the window. Looking over his shoulder, he saw Trace. Letting the window down, Kevin gave Trace a sheepish smile, and said, "Sorry, we had to clear up a couple of things."

Trace hated to interrupt, realizing Kevin and Lilly needed to talk and there had not been time before they left the cabin. However, Captain Smith had called Kevin, and he hadn't answered. "Captain Smith is at the old bike trail about a mile and a half from Safe Haven. He wants to know how far out we are."

Shifting in his seat, Kevin took out his phone, dialed Captain Smith and told him they were a little over a half an hour away. After speaking with the captain a couple of minutes more, Kevin hung up and turned to Trace, giving him a grateful smile, "Thanks, Trace. Let's get going."

Back on the highway, Kevin noticed that Lilly had retreated again to the far side of the seat. He wanted to pull her to his side, but after that amazing kiss, he knew a little distance wasn't a bad idea right now. So, he decided to bring her up to speed about what to expect when they arrived. "The place where Captain Smith is waiting for us, we call the old bike trail, but it's actually a footpath that only the Response Team members know about." Lilly's eyes lit up as she turned to face him. He continued, "I'll need you to stick close to us as we walk the trail. We have some deterrents in place in case we're ever followed, chased or have to slow someone down."

"So, you have traps? How many? Will you be able to see them in the dark? What if I trip one?"

Kevin smiled; she was excited, not scared, a very good sign. "Don't worry about the traps, just stay close to me. Once you're officially on the team, I'll show you where they all are during the day and at night." The rest of their ride was filled with questions about the team and her role as a team member. When Kevin and Trace pulled over again, they turned their headlights off, which put them in pitch darkness. They were completely off the road and under some trees with low hanging limbs. After the engines were off, all Lilly could hear were the wood creatures and her breathing, her adrenaline spiking from fear and excitement.

Fifty yards away off to the right; they saw three flashes of light, then two, then one. Kevin said, "That's Captain Smith. Let's go." Trace and Maggie emerged from the other truck, and together they walked toward the spot where the light had come from.

≈≈≈

T.J. couldn't figure out how Captain Smith knew Hector was in town. He had scoped this place out last night, and it was clear. Tonight police were everywhere, after knocking out three Resting Place police officers, he realized Hector was getting more than he bargained for. He really didn't care, but he didn't want Hector to see cops everywhere and run off before he had a chance to kill Weston. Knocking out those cops was T.J.'s way of clearing the path a little for Hector to get to the house. Once he stepped foot in that house, Weston would be a dead man. Smiling at that thought, T.J. and his dad faded into the darkness.

Hector and Little Joe watched the house. They didn't have any problem finding the place, and Hector was beginning to feel a little excitement in finally getting his revenge on Monica. He had decided he would take her from the house to a place where he could take care of her without interruptions. He saw the security camera, but wasn't concerned about it; one shot would take it out. Little Joe had found an old shack about a mile away in the woods, the perfect place to take care of Monica. Hector took a deep breath and slowly let it out as he whispered to himself, "Soon, sweet Monica, very soon." Now they only needed to wait until the house settled down for the night.

Chapter 18

Kevin, Trace, Lilly and Maggie sprinted through the woods, every now and then slowing, sidestepping, or crawling under things that Lilly could not see. She was grateful that her recent training had included running and strength training. Maggie had stressed to her that the size of her opponent did not matter with the techniques they used. At first, Lilly was skeptical, but after taking Trace down a couple of times, her confidence grew. She knew she might face Hector tonight and prayed that with God's help and her training she would be the one to walk away. A few minutes into their sprint, Lilly saw an old shack come into view; one that looked like a moderate wind could blow away. They entered and walked to a small closet with a hidden fingerprint access pad that opened to a tunnel leading to the storage room in the kitchen in Safe Haven. Lilly had walked into that closet countless times, never knowing what was hidden behind the tall shelf. Once in the storage room, Kevin made a long whistling sound. Then they waited.

≈≈≈

Ben and Tate saw a man knock the three officers out; their cameras also captured him gagging and tying them up. Ben notified the other officers in the area not to engage the man and reveal their location since he didn't use deadly force. He instructed them to monitor the situation and get the three men to safety as soon as possible. Half an hour later the three officers were removed and taken to the hospital to be checked out. Ben received a report that they reported massive headache, but otherwise, they were fine. One of them said he thought he heard T.J. call his name, but when he turned around he was hit over the head. Ben made sure Maria walked in front of the window, and then closed the blinds. They settled down and waited.

Ben had just closed his eyes when he heard Kevin's signal. Looking at Tate, he asked, "Did you hear that?"

Tate responded with a surprised look on his face, "What's Kevin doing here?" Standing, he headed for the kitchen. Neither Tate nor Ben saw the two men moving toward the house.

161

"Go see what's going on Tate. I'll cover here." Tate was moving to the kitchen before Ben finished talking. Ben checked his monitor, and seeing no change, he settled in his chair, waiting to see why Kevin had returned.

Tate hurried into the room, with Kevin, Trace, Maggie, and Lilly close behind. Ben gave them a questioning look before asking, "What are you all doing here?"

Kevin briefed Ben on the information Captain Smith had given him,

Then one of the monitors flicked off. Ben yelled, "Oh God! Tate, get upstairs!" Before Tate, Trace, and Kevin could reach the steps, the lights in the house went off.

Ben heard Brandy scream and was on his feet running toward the steps. Tate pulled out his phone, taking the steps two at a time. When they reached the bedroom, Brandy lay unconscious near the open window in the bedroom and Maria was gone.

Ben went to Brandy, yelling, "Kevin, get an ambulance!" Kevin turned and ran down the steps. When he was halfway down the steps, he saw the red dot on the wall, moving to his chest. Crouching down on the steps, he heard the shots, then felt the burning pain slicing through his shoulder, causing him to fall headfirst down the steps. He heard Lilly scream, and then everything went black. Tate ran down the steps to Kevin, gently moving Lilly out of the way, as she was crying over Kevin.

Ben was on the phone, alerting the officers that their security had been breached and that Officer Rodriquez had been taken. Lt. Travis Black informed him that they had two men watching the perpetrators' vehicle; the rest of the men would search the grounds. As Ben hung up the phone, he heard Brandy moan. "Brandy, honey, are you okay?" He went to her and gathered her in his arms.

"Ben." Brandy groaned reaching up to touch the lump on her head. He took her, through the window." Brandy struggled to get up, saying, "I tried to keep them here until someone came."

Holding Brandy in his arms, Ben spoke in a calm, assuring voice, "It's okay, we've got men all over these grounds. They won't get far." Ben whispered a prayer, of thanksgiving. "Can you stand? We need to get you checked out, and I need to check on Kevin. As Ben helped Brandy down the stairs, he could hear the ambulance getting closer.

Tate searched Kevin's body for wounds, Maggie ran over with a flashlight, holding it for him to see. Tate was scared, Maria was taken, and Kevin was shot and unconscious. Having difficulty controlling his emotions, he was praying for Maria's safety and for help to focus on Kevin. "Shoulder wound; it's bleeding pretty badly. We need to stop the bleeding. "Lilly, get me some towels, rags, something to put pressure on this wound." Lilly ran to the kitchen, in the dark but she knew her way around. She had left some towels folded on top of the dryer on Thursday. As she felt her way, she could hear knocking. She stopped and listened, there it was again. Lilly moved to the storage room where she could hear voices. Her blood ran cold as she heard Hector's voice. She grabbed the towels and ran back to Tate. "They took her to the shack!" She whispered.

Standing beside Maggie, Trace asked, "What?"

"They took her to the shack; I can hear them in the storage room. We'd better hurry; they were trying to wake her up. Hector was yelling at someone about giving her too much chloroform."

Trace headed for the kitchen with Lilly right behind him: in silence, they moved into the tunnel leading to the shack.

≈≈≈

Hector was enraged. She wouldn't wake up! How could he have his revenge when Monica was sound asleep? He had slapped her around, but couldn't wake her. Little Joe must have given her too much stuff. He didn't have time to wait until the stuff wore off. He would just have to kill her, put a bullet in her head. He hated this; he had waited years to kill her slowly, to punish her for betraying him, but now all he would get was to shoot her. Hector slapped her again, "Come on, Monica, wake up!"

Hector and Little Joe were standing over the woman in the corner of the room, unaware of the shadow that eased through the door and stood behind Little Joe. Hector heard a grunt then Little Joe hit the floor hard. He shone his light in that direction but saw nothing. "Who's there?" Hector said in a strained voice. "Who's there?" Hector, looked around again, and then pointed his gun at the woman's head.

Trace and Lilly were in the shack's closet; they heard the man fall to the floor and the fear in Hector's voice. Trace pointed his gun, ready to take a shot. "Trace, no. He might shoot her. Let me distract him." Lilly whispered.

Trace whispered, "Okay."

Lilly mustered her courage and said, "Hector, for a drug lord, you sure are stupid. You couldn't even kidnap the right woman."

"Monica? Monica! Where are you? Show yourself, or I'll kill her." Shining his light round the room, Hector couldn't see anyone.

Trace threw his keys across the room. Hector shot towards the keys. Then Trace took his shot, hitting Hector in his right leg. Hector grunted with pain and then grabbed the women on the floor. "I'll kill her! I'll kill her!" Hector yelled while backing toward the door.

Trace saw a man appear behind Hector when he reached the door. Hector shoved the woman towards the direction where he had heard Monica's voice. As Hector turned to run, the man behind him delivered a punch to his jaw that dropped him to the floor. He was out cold. Trace shone his light on the man, "Sam, what are you doing here?"

Sam smiled and said, "Ben asked me to hang around just in case he needed an extra pair of hands. Hey, you got a pair of cuffs on you? The

one over there is going to be out for a while,"
Sam said, pointing at Little Joe. "I found the
chloroform he used on that little lady and
decided to give him a taste of his own medicine.
This other one should be coming around in a
few minutes, and I want to make sure he doesn't
get away." Trace pulled out his cuffs and
handed them to Sam, then called Ben letting him
know that they had found Maria and that they
needed to get some men to come pick up Hector
and his man. Trace also told him that Hector
had been shot, but it wasn't a serious wound
from what he could see.

Trace asked, "What about Muller?"

Sam spoke again, "I saw Muller, his dad and
his cousin heading for the house. I didn't follow;
I couldn't leave these guys when they had a
woman with them."

Trace replied, "Thanks, Sam! You sure made
a difference in how this turned out." Sam smiled
and said nothing.

Ben's voice came across the phone again,
"Trace, as soon as the officers get there, I need
you and Lilly back here. We need to head out to
Muller's place ASAP. If he believes he's killed
Kevin and that Hector will take the fall for it, he
might try to get out of town for a while.

Trace, Maggie, and Lilly left Sam with the officers who arrived as Ben hung up the phone. Back at Safe Haven, Lilly rushed to Ben asking in a voice still charged with adrenaline, "Ben how are Kevin and Brandy?"

Ben breathed a sigh, "He lost a lot of blood, but he's okay. Brandy has a mild concussion, they're keeping her overnight."

Lilly whispered, "Thank you, Lord." Then she asked, "Can I see him?"

Ben replied, "Yes, you can. Now that we have Hector and his accomplice, I think it will be okay, but you'll still be under escort. Maggie, I know you want to see your mom, so if you can escort Lilly to Resting Place Memorial, Tate will stay with her while you visit your mom."

Maggie replied, "Okay, that sounds good, and Lilly can stay with me until we can locate another safe house for her." As they started to leave, Maggie turned to Trace and said, "Be careful, Cowboy." Smiling, she walked out the front door, closing it softly behind her, leaving Trace standing with a goofy smile on his face.

≈≈≈

Forty minutes later, the four uniformed police officers Ben had called for additional backup had arrived from Peace Falls, located about 30 miles south of Resting Place. They parked a few blocks away and surrounded Tim Mueller's house. Ben and Trace were crouched down under an open window on the side of the house. They could hear the three men laughing and talking about how they had bested Hector. T.J. laughed at how he got rid of Weston, and Hector was going to get blamed for it.

Ben started to give the signal for the men to move in when he heard Tim Muller say, "Yeah, that boy was just like his daddy. I had to get rid of him. It cost me my new truck, but it was worth it. He had just been promoted; and I vowed I would never work for him. Tom Hart was just supposed to push them off the road. You know, a few broken bones, but he was so drunk that he ran them into a tree and killed them both. I had just bought that truck, but it was worth it." Rage welled up inside Ben's chest. He knew something wasn't right about Kevin and Dotty's death, but he wasn't allowed to investigate the accident. Tim Muller had investigated it.

Ben felt Trace's hand on his shoulder. Leaning close, Trace whispered, "Ben, let God deal with them. I know how you feel right now,

169

and I am right there with you, but God has got to handle this, and we have to do our job." Ben took several deep breaths and prayed under his breath. Then he nodded and gave the signal to move in.

The front and the back doors were kicked in at the same time. The three men jumped up to make a run for it but found that they were surrounded. Muttering under his breath, Tim Muller raised his hands in surrender. T.J. started yelling, "What's going on here?" Roy Grimes just stood with his hands in the air.

Trace responded to T.J., "You are under arrest for the attempted murder of Officer Kevin Weston, and for the kidnapping of a federal agent. Tim Muller, you are under arrest for the murder of Kevin and Dotty Weston. Officer Black, read these men their rights. We'll be transporting them to the station."

Ben and Trace followed the two police cars to Resting Place Police Station, assisted in the intake process, and completed the necessary paperwork before heading to the hospital.

≈≈≈

Hector stood outside of Resting Place Memorial Hospital, his leg burning with pain. The

paramedic had attended to him before their
transport to Peace Falls Police Station, but the
pain medication had worn off a couple of hours
before. Hector huffed, thinking to himself he'd
been in much worse pain than this. He would be
alright. It was time to focus; he had some
unfinished business before he left town. He
smiled at how stupid these backwoods cops
were. He only had to fake passing out near the
cell door, then once the cop came over to check
on him, Hector grabbed his necktie and pulled
hard, slamming the cop's face into the bars
knocking him out. All Hector had to do was
grab the keys and walk out of the cell. Once
free, he took the policeman's gun and picked his
pockets for money, taking some bills. Hector
thought about finding Little Joe but decided it
would take too much time. He couldn't risk
getting caught again, and he still had to deal
with Monica. Laughing at how gullible these
country cops were, Hector limped out of the
police station to a nearby neighborhood looking
around for some easy transportation to get back
to Resting Place. He had overheard Monica say
she wanted to go to the hospital. He was going
to pay her another visit and this time finish what
he started.

One hour after leaving Peace Falls, Hector watched as groups of people left the hospital, going over his plan in his head. He had waited in the stolen car at the back of the parking lot to watch the hospital door. Getting out of the vehicle, he moved to a place near the corner of the building. Whoever came out of the door would have to pass him to get to the parking lot. Leaning against the brick wall, he waited.

≈≈≈

As Lilly walked into the waiting room, she saw people holding hands with their heads bowed in prayer. She had seen the way Maggie looked at Trace when no one was around. Lilly had noticed the longing in her eyes that would turn to a determined stare. Lilly knew that look well; she had often done that same thing with Kevin, allowing her heart to desire him for a split second, then steeling it to stop the longing for something that would never happen. She made up her mind that she would talk with Maggie about her doubts and fears, maybe tonight after they were settled. As she walked closer, she heard Trace end their prayer, saw him hesitate before pulling Maggie into his arms in a tight embrace. Smiling, Trace handed Maggie his keys and told her to drive his truck; he would take Kevin's vehicle. Ben was staying at the hospital to take Brandy home in the morning, so Trace could return his truck before going to work. As he turned to leave, his eyes met and held Maggie's, and for a few heartbeats, they just stared. Smiling, Trace said goodnight and walked away.

Walking over to Maggie, Lilly asked, "Ready?"

Maggie was at a loss for words; her senses were on overload with Trace Kenton. She shook her head to clear it and replied, "Yeah, I'm ready. How's Kevin doing?"

They headed for the door as Lilly responded, "He's on some strong medication, but he's good. I'm so grateful."

Walking out of the hospital, Lilly turned to ask where Trace's truck was when someone grabbed her from behind and pushed Maggie to the ground. Lilly heard the click of the gun before she heard Hector's voice.

"Stay down, pretty lady, or you won't be able to get up." Pointing the gun at Maggie, Hector started pulling Lilly toward the parking lot, whispering in her ear, "Hello, sweet Monica, did you miss me? We're going for a little ride, honey; we have some unfinished business."

Lilly, frozen for a few seconds, was unable to process that Hector had somehow escaped and found her. Then she prayed, "Father, help us! What can I do?" At that moment she felt peace come over her. She closed her eyes and went limp, falling out of Hector's one-arm hold.

As she hit the ground, she heard Trace yell, "Drop the gun!"

Opening her eyes, Lilly saw Hector turn awkwardly to fire at Trace. Thinking fast, she kicked his injured leg and rolled away from him. She heard two shots, and someone fall to the ground. Maggie ran over to Lilly, helping her to her feet. When she looked around, she saw Hector on the ground bleeding from a chest wound, not moving. Trace was kneeling beside him checking for a pulse. Then shaking his head, he took out his phone and called Ben. Turning to Maggie, Trace asked if she was okay and told her to take Lilly back inside until the police came. As Lilly walked back to the hospital, tears began to fall; she couldn't stop them, tears of release. All she kept saying was, "Thank You, God." It was over.

Epilogue

Three months later Lilly was getting dressed for the wedding of Kevin's youngest brother Marcus and Stephanie, Sidney's best friend's. Lilly marveled at how much her life had changed in the past few months. She had become best friends with Sidney, Stephanie, and Maggie. Best friends! Something she had never had before. She and Kevin were engaged. Kevin had surprised her at Marcus and Stephanie's rehearsal dinner the night before, getting down on one knee and asking her to marry him. She could barely breathe; she was so excited and happy. When she could say yes, he kissed her; she still turned pink just thinking about it.

Lilly gazed at her ring, thanking God for her new life. Brandy had offered her the manager's position at Safe Haven last month before her wedding to Ben Rayns. Touching her locket with Ricardo's picture, she whispered, "It's over, Rico; Hector can't hurt anyone else." Lilly could almost picture him grinning, and saying, "You did good, Sis." Smiling, she checked her watch and ran into the bathroom to put on her makeup.

≈≈≈

Kevin was early, but he couldn't wait any longer; he wanted to be with Lilly. These past three months had been heaven for him. He thanked God every day for his relationship with Lilly. She was so amazing. He also thanked God for Trace and his Holy Spirit alert system. Trace told him that after he had left the hospital that night, the farther he drove, the more his spirit was troubled. He turned around, drove back and saw Hector dragging Lilly away. "Thank you, Jesus," Kevin whispered.

Kevin and Lilly had decided to wait until after his brother's wedding before making plans for theirs. Grams was on cloud nine. She was in her element, planning and fussing over wedding plans. She had coordinated Ben and Brandy's small wedding, and that had just seemed to energize her. Since their engagement, Grams had been asking questions about what colors they wanted and how big the wedding should be. Kevin just smiled and said, "Whatever Lilly wants." However, he did want something that he had to talk with her about. He did not want a long engagement, and he hoped that Lilly felt the same way, too, but that was a conversation for after this wedding. Pulling up at Safe Haven, he parked and walked to the door, ringing the bell and straightening his bowtie.

When Lilly opened the door, Kevin lost his breath. This woman was absolutely gorgeous! Pulling her into his arms, Kevin whispered, "God, you do all things well."

Lilly pulled back and asked, "What did you say? I didn't hear you."

"You look beautiful."

Smiling, Lilly said, "You look great, too." Taking his offered arm, they walked to Kevin's truck.

Lilly seemed a little shy. Kevin helped her into the truck and walked around to get in before asking, "What's up? Is something on your mind?"

She was quiet for a few seconds, but the silence seemed much longer. Then she just blurted it out, "I know we said we would wait until after Marcus' wedding to talk about ours, but I don't want to wait. I want to get married as soon as we can."

Kevin asked, "Are you sure? It's not the money, Lilly; we can afford a big wedding."

Lilly took a deep breath and replied, "I want the kind of wedding that Ben and Brandy had, small and intimate. I don't have any family left, and I just want to be your family."

Grinning, Kevin asked, "Did you bring your makeup with you?"

Lilly looked puzzled, "Yes, why?"

"Because, my beautiful soon-to-be-bride, I love you so much and I don't want to wait either, and I am about to mess up your makeup." Then Kevin lowered his head and kissed her.

Dear Reader,

I hope you enjoyed reading *Resting Place: Safe Haven* as much as I enjoyed writing it.

The characters in this book were dear to me because as a young adult, I was a victim of domestic violence. Verbal and mental abuse can leave behind wounds that we carry long after the physical abuse has ended.

It is my sincere hope that through these characters' struggles and ultimate success that someone will be encouraged and seek Him who heals, restores and affirms, as He did for me. Truly God is a strong tower that we can run to and be safe.

Thank you for reading *Resting Place: Safe Haven*! If you would like to find out what happens with Trace and Maggie, check out my next book called *Resting Place: Guardians*!

Blessings to you!
Mary Beasley

For the latest news on releases and book sales of Mary Beasley, visit www.lminow.com.